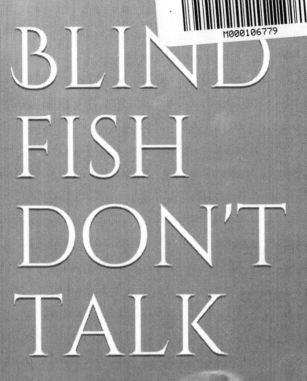

BLIND
FISH
DON'T
TALK

A Julia Fairchild Mystery

PJ Peterson

Enjoy!
PJ Peterson

ABOUT
BLIND FISH DON'T TALK

Dr. Julia Fairchild was planning to enjoy a romantic Caribbean holiday with her new flame, Tony. She envisioned days lying on the beach, reading murder mysteries, and doing some scuba diving. Plans changed when he couldn't join her right away, and she stumbled onto a dead scuba diver. No one else seemed to think that it might not be an accidental death. Julia's sixth sense told her otherwise. And doctors are really detectives at heart.

BLIND FISH DON'T TALK

A Julia Fairchild Mystery

PJ PETERSON

BLIND FISH DON'T TALK
Copyright © 2018 by PJ Peterson. All rights reserved.

AUTHOR'S NOTE

I love to write! I've been writing poems and short stories since grade school. I have had non-clinical articles published in *Medical Economics,* and clinical journal articles related to my medical background published in the medical literature. More recently I have written short stories specifically for some of my great-nieces and great-nephews. For the last several years, I have also been an outside reviewer for *On Being A Doctor* in *Annals of Internal Medicine.* Just last year I won a local Haiku contest, winning the grand prize for traditional Haiku.

This novel began as an entry in my travel journal many years ago. It somehow morphed into a story, then into a bigger manuscript. At the time, fear of rejection, having to find an agent and lack of time while working and raising a family kept it from going beyond a Word 97 document on a floppy disc. Then some cosmic force intervened. While vacationing in Italy I met a fellow writer (Lori Hicks, from Phoenix AZ) in Rome. We were waiting in line to go into the Vatican and somehow started talking about writing. She told me about self-publishing and Createspace.com. I looked at that website as soon as I returned home.

A few more years passed, but when I finally retired from my full-time medical practice, I decided it was time to take this plunge. I had earlier promised my father (who has since died in 2006) that I would get my murder mystery published and I wanted to keep my word to him.

Some of the incidents in my novel are actual events, such as my arrival at the first hotel, the catamaran sail to St. Bart's, and the limbo contest. Details, of course, are modified for this story. Most of the rest of the novel came from some mysterious place in my brain! For example, I didn't know if blind fish actually existed at the time I

4

wrote this, but I "invented" them so Linda would have a reason to go into that cave. There are probably real people who share some of the names in the story, but, trust me, the characters are totally fictional!

My second 'Julia Fairchild' novel is in the works. I am confident that it will not sit on my desk as long as this one did. In the meantime, I have a note on the mirror above my desk for my friends that says, "Careful or you'll end up in my novel."

I hope you enjoy reading "Blind Fish Don't Talk."

PJ Peterson

DEDICATION

This murder mystery is dedicated to my wonderful father, Rudolph N. Kangas. He and my mother, Martha, raised me and my five siblings with kindness and love. Though he didn't have the opportunity to go beyond high school himself, he was ahead of his time in insisting that his four daughters get college educations. He wanted us to be able to take care of ourselves instead of having to be dependent on someone else. He also encouraged us to wait until the age of twenty-one to get married. We all abided by his wishes.

He was a man of relatively few words, but what he did say was well-thought out and wise. He regularly read 'Time', 'Newsweek' and 'U.S. News and World Reports', as well as mostly non-fiction novels. I still 'hear' his words of wisdom in my daily life.

I promised him that I would get this novel published, some day.

Thank you, Dad, for instilling a love of reading by your example, and for your support of higher education. And for teaching us that we could be anything we wanted to be, if we worked hard enough.

With love,

Your Daughter, PJ (Patricia Joan Kangas) Peterson

CONTENTS

CHAPTER ONE

Welcome to Paradise

Julia was a little apprehensive as she stepped outside the baggage claim area to the line of cabs. All the men were friendly and helpful, but she was alone and somewhat concerned about her safety. Five minutes earlier she had been worried that one of her suitcases had missed the flight. She thought of every possible mishap before she finally spotted it, sitting all by itself on the floor next to the carousel.

Relieved, she moved outside to the curb and scanned the area looking for a blond woman. There was supposed to have been a friend of Tony's at the airport to meet her, but no one identified herself and no one seemed to be left over when all the people on the flight were claimed, so Julia set out for the next task, which is what caused her to have to hail a cab.

Her driver was explaining the island people and asking her questions about where she was from, and if she was alone. Everyone seemed surprised that she traveled alone. How long had it been since she started traveling solo? Seven years? It was easy now, but it had only come with experience—some good, some bad. She hoped this would be one of those good ones.

Finally, the driver stopped in front of a tired old building. He announced that this was the *Caribbean Hotel.*

She didn't see any hotel signs and asked the driver, "Where?" He pointed in the direction of some stairs. This certainly did not look like the "luxury hotel in downtown Phillipsburg" advertised in the brochures. What next?

Once she found her way up the stairs, she discovered that there was no one at the desk. Two other people (a couple) were waiting in the small dark lobby. It appeared that construction was going on. Someone located the disco owner downstairs. He relayed the information that the hotel manager was out for the night on the French side of the island. It was Friday night, after all. Julia had a feeling of panic, but the other couple seemed pretty calm, so she decided not to worry. She was tired, however, and longed for a bed, as it was now well after midnight.

Finally, a young black girl in curlers came padding downstairs from an upper floor. She jumped over the registration desk and seemed to know what she was doing. Julia paid for the room and was directed down the hall. All she cared about was a bed, but she wasn't really prepared for what she saw upon opening the door. The room was all of 6 feet square with one big sagging bed, one small bathroom, and no lock on the door. Julia's dream of a wonderful Caribbean vacation was quickly dissolving. She told herself that everything would work out in the morning, crawled into the bed and promptly fell asleep.

The next morning, she was startled from deep sleep as the door opened. The young man, who turned out to be the proprietor, apologized as Julia stared at him. Her first morning on her trip and she couldn't even sleep in! What a welcome to the Caribbean!

After quickly showering and dressing, she hopped outside and marveled at the hundreds (at least it seemed like hundreds) of shops along the main street. Traffic went one way down the narrow cobblestone lane. The shops were crowded next to each other, and even behind one another in some alleys. Everyone was trying to sell cameras, watches, stereos, radios, linens, gold jewelry, t-shirts, and souvenirs.

Then she saw the turquoise water with a cruise ship at anchor in the bay and Julia felt all her apprehension slip away. It would be wonderful, surely, after all.

• • •

Julia Fairchild lived and worked in a small town in Washington state. She had her own clinic and had worked hard all her life to be able to afford nice things, travel, and hoped, eventually, to have a big beautiful house with a handsome husband, three children, and maybe a maid. She smiled as she thought about that.

An earlier marriage hadn't worked out, although she remained optimistic that some day in the future she would meet "the one." Realistically, the opportunities for meeting eligible men in her own community were practically non-existent for young professionals. For now, Julia was here to have fun and to take advantage of an earlier chance meeting with Tony.

Something had attracted her to him at the hotel in Monterey, California, where she had been attending a conference. Maybe it was the nice body with quality clothes and a friendly posture. Maybe it was the brown wavy hair and gorgeous blue eyes. Or maybe it had been the way he smiled at her when he caught her staring at him. He appeared to be in his early 30's, tanned and relaxed.

"Can I help you, Miss?" He was talking to her!

"Oh, I'm sorry. I was daydreaming and didn't realize you were standing there. I was just trying to figure out this silly schedule."

"What kind of a schedule?"

"It's a schedule of my meetings."

"Oh. So, you're here on business also."

"Yes, I'm here for a seminar. You know, one of those continuing-education sessions."

"Well, welcome to Monterey. If you need any information, I'll be glad to help. My name is Tony Romero. I have business that brings me here frequently and know the area quite well." He glanced over Julia's shoulder and said, "Oh, there's my associate now. I have an appointment in a few minutes, but perhaps we could meet for a drink later?"

Julia was pinching herself. This couldn't be real. "I'd love to." Who wouldn't?

"Alright. Let's make it 7 o'clock at the bar upstairs. And your name?"

"Julia. Julia Fairchild."

"Julia. Lovely. Seven o'clock then. Ciao." He smiled and waved as he walked off with the new arrival.

That had been three months ago. Life hadn't been the same since. Tony seemed to be made of money. She had flown to Chicago, San Francisco, and Dallas to meet him. He would call and ask if she were free, arrange for her tickets, and wine and dine her wherever they happened to be. She had been disappointed that he couldn't meet her in St. Maarten. It had been planned to be a holiday trip for both of them but he had been unable to get away at the last minute. However, he insisted that she go anyway to deliver some papers for him and he had given her names of some friends of his for company while she was there.

So here she was. Her first night hadn't been that wonderful, but she was expected at one of the island's nicest hotels for the next 10 days. And the sun was shining. She wouldn't even think about anything but working on a suntan for the next few days, once she delivered Tony's manila envelope.

Later that morning, she collected her belongings and took a taxi to the Mullet Bay Hotel.

"Excuse me, sir," she said at the hotel registration desk.

"Yes, mademoiselle," replied a young man.

"I'd like to register for my room. I have a reservation in the name of Julia Fairchild."

He ascertained that everything was in order and gave here the room key, with arrangements made to bring her luggage up later.

Julia was delighted with the room. She had a wonderful view of the Caribbean to the west. Everything was done in very good taste in soft blue and beige colors. There were thick towels in the bathroom and a big fluffy robe as well.

Her first order of business was to contact Tony's friend, Linda. She found the number, courtesy of Tony, and dialed. No answer. She was a little perturbed because Linda was supposed to have met her at the airport, and now wasn't even available at home. Julia really wanted to get the papers to her as soon as possible to fulfill her obligation.

Julia decided to rent a car and deliver the envelope personally. Tony had given her Linda's work address as well as home address, in case Julia might need them. Once that was out of the way, she could enjoy the rest of the week.

The map of the island was not nearly as exact as U.S. maps, so Julia had a little difficulty finding the address. She parked, and then knocked on the door of the small green house. There was mail addressed to Linda Townsend in the box on the porch, but no answer to her knocking, so Julia left a note with the mail and went to the work address. It was a dive shop, and chances were she was still at work, being that it was a Saturday, which is typically a busy day for diving.

Fifteen minutes later, she pulled up in front of Underwater Sports. She entered the small shop, which seemed even smaller because of all the clutter—windsurf boards, scuba tanks, BC (buoyancy compensator) vests, masks, fins, snorkels, and boxes were piled all over. There were two customers checking on some tanks, and a tanned gentleman examining an underwater camera set-up. Julia planned to do some diving while here, so she decided to kill two birds with one visit while she could. She walked over to a clerk who didn't appear to be busy with customers.

"Is Linda Townsend working here today?" she asked the young blond male at the main register.

"She's supposed to be here today, but we haven't seen her. It's funny, too, because she had a lesson this morning and she never misses a lesson, so someone else had to do it instead."

"You mean she just didn't show up? Didn't she call or anything?"

"Well, our line has been out of order since yesterday, so it's possible she got tied up at St. Barthelemy yesterday and couldn't get word to us. Could I help you?"

"Oh, I'm sorry. I should explain. Linda and I have a mutual friend and he asked me to deliver a package to her. And now I'm trying to locate her."

"Did you try her house?"

"I was there a little while ago. There was no one home. I saw mail in her box, but I couldn't tell if it was yesterday's or today's."

"We don't get mail delivered on Saturday, so it must be Friday's mail. She probably just got tied up at St. Bart's with the dive job she was doing yesterday. Do you want to leave that package here for her? I'll be happy to take care of it."

"Thanks, but I'd rather take care of it personally. You can give her a message, though, to contact me at my hotel. If you've got a piece of paper, I'll leave my name and a number." Julia wrote a short note and handed it to him. "By the way, I'm going to be doing some diving while I'm here. How hard is it to arrange for a private guide?"

"We have a lot of them. I just need a day's notice to line you up. When did you want to dive?"

"Probably not until Tuesday at the earliest. I hope to do some sailing on Monday."

"Fine. Just check with us on Monday and we can take care of details then."

"Super! Thanks a lot."

"You're welcome, uh, Julia," he said, as he glanced at the message she'd left. "My name is Scott. I hope you enjoy your stay on the Friendly Island."

"Thanks, I'm sure I will." Especially with handsome men like him around, she thought to herself.

CHAPTER TWO

Damsels in Distress

Julia was anxious to get rid of Tony's package, but since she couldn't locate Linda, she decided to enjoy the sun for a while instead and headed back to the hotel.

The sun was warm, the breeze was comfortable, and the water perfect at the beach right at the hotel. She swam for a few minutes, then stretched out on the beach to work on her tan. She was suddenly aware that someone was standing over her. She looked up to see a good-looking male smiling down at her.

"Hello. You must be from the north country with skin that light." His voice was nice, too, with a British accent.

Julia smiled back, "Yes, I am, but I tan fast."

"Mind if I join you?"

"Not at all."

He sat down on his towel and continued, "My name is Ian McDonnell. Who are you and where are you from?"

"My name is Julia. I'm from Washington. The state, that is, and I'm pleased to meet you."

"Washington! You're a long way from home. What caused you to come way down here?"

"A friend suggested it. He said it was better than Hawaii. So I'm trying it out."

"So, you're here with a friend, then?"

"No. I was supposed to be here with a friend, but he had some business that kept him from coming on schedule. But he will join me later in the week."

"So that means you're here alone for the time being?"

"Yes, for now. I'm planning to do lots of tanning and enjoy being away from work until he gets here."

"A pretty girl like you shouldn't have any trouble having fun,"he smiled.

Julia blushed. That was one thing she couldn't control.

"How long have you been here?" he continued.

"I just arrived here last night and will be here for a week.What about you?"

"I live here now. I moved here about four years ago and have my own business on the island now."

"Then you might know the girl I've been trying to get in touch with. Her name is Linda Townsend." Julia was excited.

"Linda? The one who works at Underwater Sports?"

"Yes, that's her."

"Yes, I know her. She's done some work for me, in fact. Did you try her at work?"

"Yes. They said she didn't come in today and there was no one at her house. Scott at the dive shop said he thought she might have gotten delayed at St. Barthelemy yesterday on a job she was doing."

"No, she didn't."

"How do you know that? Have you seen her?"

"She was doing a dive for me yesterday and we finished up before noon."

"Did she come back with you?"

"No, she had her boat and said she had some things to do and would return a little later."

"Her mail from Friday was still in her mailbox. She must not have returned yet. Does she have a boyfriend who might know if she got back?"

"No one steady, but she had been seeing a lot of Martin Thompson recently. He might know. Do you want to talk to him?"

"Please. Can you tell me how to get in touch with him?"

"Better than that, I'll take you there. Do you need to change?"

"Yes. My suit is wet."

"Okay. I'll wait for you to change and we can go over together."

They walked back to the hotel. Ian headed for a phone to make a call as Julia rushed up to change into dry clothes.

Thirty minutes later, they pulled up in Ian's white Mercedes in front of a modest house near Simpson Bay. A knock on the door was answered promptly by a slightly built man with a big moustache and wavy brown hair.

"Ian, hello! What a surprise!" The accent was British. That made two so far. "Come in!"

"Martin, I'd like you to meet Julia...Julia..."

"Fairchild," Julia added.

"Thank you. Julia, this is Martin Thompson. He's one of the local authorities on the island. In fact, he's in charge of law enforcement on the Dutch side."

"Nice to meet you."

"What brings you here, Ian?" Martin asked.

"Actually, Julia is the one who wants to talk to you."

Julia nodded in agreement. "I was supposed to meet Linda Townsend at the airport yesterday but I haven't been able to find her. Do you know where she is?"

"Why, yes. I talked to her last night. She said she was staying at St. Bart's and would return today."

"She hasn't been back yet."

"Well, I wouldn't worry about her. She probably decided to do some diving there today or something. She can be quite unpredictable."

"Well, at least we know where she is. Thanks anyway."

Julia and Ian turned and left. Julia was deep in thought. She didn't know what it was that kept nagging her, but some sixth sense told her that she had to keep looking. "Ian, is it too late to fly to St. Bart's today?"

He looked at his watch. "No, there's a flight in about 45 minutes. You could catch it easily. Would you like me to go with you? It might be helpful to have a guide who is familiar with the island."

"That would be nice. But you don't have to. After all, this is my problem."

"It's always a pleasure to help pretty ladies in distress. He smiled that gorgeous smile again. "Let's go."

It was only a short hop in a small twin-engine Cessna from St. Maarten to St. Bart's. The runway headed straight toward the water as they descended. Julia caught her breath as they finally stopped. She silently wondered how many planes had kept on going into the Caribbean. She resolved not to ask. Ian rented a car from a friendly Frenchman who appeared to have a monopoly on the rental car business. There were at least 30 identical little Renaults parked at his airport lot, albeit in different colors.

It was then just a short drive up and down through the beautiful country-side on a narrow road to the capital city. Gustavia was popular with boaters because of its natural sheltered harbor, Ian explained. Although St. Bart's was now a part of France, the island had once been controlled by Sweden and many of the Swedish names had been retained.

Once at the marina, Ian asked the owner if he had seen Linda since the day before.

"She hasn't been here. When she left yesterday, she said she was going on to check on her fish."

"Her fish?", asked Julia.

Ian explained, "She was studying some fish in an underwater cave on the island. She apparently had a degree in biology and was working on a Master's thesis while supporting herself with diving jobs."

19

"Do you know where the cave is?" asked Julia.

"I've heard her talk about it and I know the general location."

Julia interrupted, "I want to go there."

"Do you dive?"

"Yes, and I want to go find this cave. Linda could be in trouble there."

"She's an excellent diver. I doubt she's in trouble. Besides, it's too late to dive today. I'd never find the cave in this light. We better wait until tomorrow. And she might even be home by now."

Ian added, "Her boat's not here. I think we should go back to St. Maarten and I'm sure she'll be there."

Julia wanted to believe that would be the case, so she consented. They thanked Tom, the owner, and hurried back to the airport to catch the last plane of the day back to St. Maarten.

Once back on St. Maarten, Julia and Ian drove to Linda's house. There was a light on in the back. Julia noticed that the mail was no longer there. There was still no response when they knocked on the door, however.

Ian broke the momentary silence. "She's probably just out. After all, it is Saturday. And she always leaves a light on at night. Look, Julia. I'll take you back to your hotel and you get a good night's sleep. I'll take care of looking for Linda tonight."

Julia was too tired to argue. Jet lag was a bit of a problem. There was a time difference of four hours from her home and she had gotten less than a normal night's sleep after a long day of traveling. After a short drive, Ian pulled up to the entrance of the hotel.

"How about it if I meet you for breakfast tomorrow?" Ian asked.

"That would be fine."

"About 8?"

"Perfect. I'll jog in the morning and still have plenty of time to get ready."

Ian planted a small kiss on her forehead.

"Ian, thanks for helping me try to find Linda today. You didn't have to do that!"

"Like I said, I like helping damsels in distress!" He smiled and waved and left.

Julia had to smile. He was a nice person and she found herself wondering if he might be free for an evening or two. In her room a few minutes later, she was ready for bed. She decided to wait to call Tony in the morning because she hadn't seen Linda yet anyway.

She sat down to write a summary of the day's events in her travel diary, as was her habit, before falling into bed, exhausted.

CHAPTER THREE

Where's Linda?

The sun was shining brightly into the room. Julia had not slept well, again. She'd had nightmares of divers being gobbled up by sea anemones.

She dragged herself out of bed, pulled on her jogging clothes, and went out to greet the morning. She was about half way through her three-mile run when she met another runner coming from the opposite direction. She decided to turn around and head back to the hotel as they met.

"Good morning! So, I'm not the only crazy runner around here", Julia said as she greeted the other woman.

"Hi. You must be new here. Are you on vacation?", she replied as she stepped in stride with Julia.

"Yes, I am," Julia replied.

"Where are you staying?" asked the new jogger.

"At Mullet Bay."

"Oh, that's nice," said the other jogger. "You must have a lot of money to stay there."

"Not me! My boyfriend is paying for it. He was supposed to come with me but I ended up coming by myself at the last minute," Julia explained.

"Do you know anybody here, then?"

Julia replied, "Only a man that I met here yesterday. I also have a name to contact for my boyfriend. You wouldn't be Linda Townsend, by any chance, would you?"

"No. I'm Jill Sorensen. But I do know Linda. We've done a lot of diving together."

"Oh really? I tried to find her yesterday, but wasn't able to connect. I guess I'll go over to her house later again. By the way, I'm Julia Fairchild. You mentioned diving. Do you know anything about Linda's cave and her fish?"

"No, not really. I heard she was going into a cave on St. Bart's, but that's all. Why?"

"I was just curious. I've never been in an underwater cave before. I wonder what it's like."

"It can be kinda spooky if you don't like enclosed places, but it's also quite a neat experience."

"Well, maybe I'll try it someday. Do you get to dive often?" Julia asked.

"It depends. I used to teach scuba full-time, but now I only do private guide work in my spare time. I have a full-time job at the hotel doing the tourist service."

"That sounds like a great combination. I had planned to do some diving here. In fact, I talked to Scott at Underwater Sports about a private guide for Tuesday. Would you be interested in diving with me that day?"

Jill replied, "Sure. That's my day off anyway. I'd be glad to."

"Wonderful! That's terrific!" Julia was excited. They approached the hotel and slowed down to a walk to cool down.

Julia asked, "Do you run every day?"

"I try to. Would you be interested in running together while you're here? I run about this time every day."

"I'd love it. Do you want to meet here at the hotel? Say 6:30 A.M.?"

"Sounds good".

"Great. Jill, I'll see you tomorrow. Thanks for the run."

Julia waved good-bye as Jill headed for her apartment down the road. Julia felt invigorated after her run. She mentally planned her day, beginning with seeing Linda after breakfast with Ian, and headed for the shower.

Ian impatiently watched for Julia to waltz through the door of the restaurant. He had already had one 'Sweetheart' (a local bar drink) and was working on his second when he spotted her. She walked to his table, long brown hair still slightly damp.

Ian spoke first. "Good morning, Julia. You look bright and chipper today."

"Hello, yourself. What are you drinking? Instant Breakfast?" She was pointing to his drink. Julia sat down next to him.

"No, it's a specialty drink that the bartender here makes. Tastes like strawberries and coconut, with a little rum. Here, try it."

"No, thanks. Orange juice is more my speed," she giggled.

"Well, Julia, did you get your jog in? Or did you sleep in?" Ian winked.

"Oh, I had a great run. I even met somebody while I was running."

"Oh really? Male or female?" He acted a little jealous.

"Actually, female. Another runner. Jill Sorenson. Do you know her?"

"Not well."

"Well, we decided to run together in the mornings and she said she'd dive with me on Tuesday. I'm really excited about that!"

The waiter finally came to take their order. Julia spoke up after he left the table. "Ian, did you talk to Linda last night?"

"Uh, no. I couldn't find her, but I didn't look very hard. There are a lot of places she could have been." Ian didn't seem particularly worried.

"I'm going to go over to her house as soon as we finish breakfast, then."

"What is so damned important about talking to Linda?" Ian asked.

"I have some papers to give her from Tony, my friend at home. He said they have something to do with business and to get them to her ASAP."

"What kind of papers could be that important?"

"I'm not sure. I just know I need to deliver them." Julia insisted.

"Okay, next question, Julia. What kind of business is Tony in?"

"Wholesale importing and distributorships."

"I see. So, what will you do if you can't find Linda today?"

At that point, breakfast arrived, smelling delicious.

"I'm sure I'll find her today. I left her a message to contact me here. Anyway, as soon as I've done my business, I can concentrate on enjoying my vacation. Umm, this is delicious!"

Some thirty minutes later, Julia said her good-byes, hopped into her spiffy little rental Toyota Corolla and headed for Linda's house, once again. Once there, she knocked on the door. No answer. She peered into the living room window but didn't see anyone. Undaunted, she went around to the back. The light that she'd seen the day before was still on.

Julia was getting a little worried. She tried the door but it was locked. She could see a pile of papers and mail on the kitchen table. She couldn't understand why Linda hadn't contacted her. After a moment of thought, she decided to find Jill. Another fifteen minutes later, after getting Jill's address from the hotel manager, Julia knocked at Jill's door.

"Julia, what a surprise. What are you doing here?"

Julia answered, "Jill, could you dive today?"

"I suppose so, I don't have anything important scheduled. What's up?"

"I still can't find Linda and I'm worried. I don't think she was home last night. The last time anyone talked to her was Friday night, possibly Saturday, and she said she'd be home Saturday night, according to Martin. I think she might be in trouble, maybe in her cave. I'd like to go there and see if we can find her."

"Gee, I don't know exactly where her cave is, but there are only three on the island that I know of. Two are very small and barely big enough for a human, so we should try the largest one first. We'll have to go over to St. Bart's. I loaned my boat out, so we'll have to borrow one. Yeah, I'll be glad to help. She's a good diver, though, and probably just stayed over."

Julia responded, "I'd rather know for sure. I'll need to borrow some gear. I only brought my fins, mask and snorkel with me."

"No problem. I'll take care of everything we'll need. Can you meet me at Bobby's Marina in maybe an hour? Do you know where that is?"

"Yes, right by Underwater Sports. I'll be there at 10:30." Jill smiled and waved as Julia walked toward her car, climbed in and drove off. Julia hoped they'd find the right cave. How would they know if they did? She suddenly realized that this might be more difficult than she originally thought. Once back at the hotel, she stopped at the desk to see if Linda had answered her message.

"Hello, Miss Fairchild. I do have two messages for you. One from a man named Tony Romero. He wants you to call him back tonight. And Ian asked you to meet him at 7:00 P.M. for dinner."

"Nothing from Linda Townsend?"

"No, Mademoiselle. Just those two."

"Okay, thank you." She smiled and headed for her room. She considered telling Ian she was going diving and might be late, but decided against it. She was certain she'd be back in time. And she didn't want him to talk her out of going. There was no answer at Tony's when she tried his number.

Another half hour later, Julia and Jill anchored the small runabout about 150 feet off shore of St Bart's Island. They reviewed their hand signals, made final equipment checks, and went into the water.

Julia was excited about the warm water. She was accustomed to diving in 40-degree water in Hood Canal, which is west of Puget Sound in Washington state, and had dreamed of diving in such wonderful warm water. It was even better than she'd imagined. The fish were very brilliantly colored, more so than at home. She saw big blue fish which looked like giant gouramis, yellow and black fish that looked like the old CBS "eye," small blue and pink striped fish and huge yellow tangs. She wished she had a camera with her.

Jill was leading the way toward a shallow opening in the wall ahead. Julia followed her into a six- by six-foot shaft which sloped upwards. Only a few minutes later they were in a huge open room underground. Julia and Jill surfaced and surveyed the room. It was at least 20 feet across, with an irregular shape. Julia's flashlight made eerie shadows on the walls and ceiling because of the rough, rocky surface.

Jill spoke first, "Well, I don't see anything here."

Julia went around a dark corner and let out a shriek. "Jill, come here. Quickly!"

Jill swam to the darkened corner, not believing what she saw when she joined Julia. A diver was lying face down in the shallow water, mask and mouthpiece still in place. No respiration. No pulse.

"It's Linda, isn't it," Julia asked, knowing the answer.

"Yes, but I don't understand. She's got plenty of air according to the gauge." She breathed on Linda's mouthpiece, "and I get plenty of air now. She must have had some kind of mechanical problem. It looks like she shouldn't have been diving alone this time."

Julia volunteered, "Maybe there was an equipment failure? Maybe she got into trouble and came up too fast? Maybe she had an air embolus?"

"Anything could have happened. I can't believe this. Do you think you can manage her tank if I take care of getting the body to the boat?" Jill asked Julia.

"Yes, of course. I wonder what Tony will say when I tell him about this."

Julia and Jill proceeded with the preparations to return with Linda's body and gear to the boat. It was a sad trip motoring to Gustavia.

CHAPTER FOUR

In Limbo

After giving an account of what had happened to the French authorities on St. Bart's, Julia tried to call Ian to cancel dinner. There was no answer at his home.

Julia and Jill left Linda's body on St. Bart's and headed home to St. Maarten. Although the body had been found on St Bart's island, because Linda lived on St. Maarten, arrangements were made for St. Maarten authorities to pick up her body on Monday. Julia was anxious to talk to Ian or Martin. It was always bad publicity to have a diver die, but especially so when it was so near tourist season.

Martin was waiting to talk to her when she got back to the hotel.

"Julia, I'm sorry this had to happen," were his first words.

Julia started to bawl as he put his arms around her. She asked if Linda's family had been contacted when she finally regained her composure.

"Yes, they were apparently planning to visit anyway and will be here late Monday morning."

"Maybe an autopsy will show what happened", Julia mused.

"It looks pretty straight forward. Equipment failure, most likely. Diver alone. I don't think we need one this time," Martin replied.

"But there was air in the tank. Maybe she stayed underwater too long and got the bends," Julia offered.

"We, I mean, I didn't ask her family if they wanted one."

"But you're the authority and could order one on the basis of the circumstances," Julia protested.

"Why are you so set on an autopsy? It was an accident. Things happen. Divers get careless." Martin sounded a bit sharp.

"I just think it would be nice to know for sure. She might have had an air embolus, or something else unexpected. Besides, I'm a doctor and I believe in autopsies in questionable cases."

"You! A doctor? You look much too young to be a doctor. What kind?" Martin was clearly surprised.

"Internal Medicine specialist. And I've done some study in diving medicine. This could even be important for other divers. We always learn from autopsies." Julia was pleading by this time. "If you don't mind, I'm going to ask her family if they would agree to an autopsy."

"But I already told them she didn't need one."

"That's okay. I'll explain my reasons," Julia replied.

"But we'll have all her equipment checked. I think that will be enough,"

Martin offered.

"That's essential, too," Julia said as she smiled, sensing that she had won the argument.

Martin didn't look very happy. For one brief moment Julia wondered if there was a reason he didn't want the autopsy, but dismissed that thought. She noticed the clock on the wall. It read 6:20. She had just enough time to shower and change for dinner with Ian. She was glad she would have company for dinner this evening.

Julia broke the silence. "If you don't have any more questions, I'd like to excuse myself and get ready for dinner."

"No. No more questions. I still want to talk to Jill tonight. Thanks for your help, Julia. I'm sure sorry you had to get involved in this."

Martin offered his hand as he rose to go to the door. Julia noticed his choice of words, but let it pass as he exited her room. Now she needed to talk to Tony and see what she was supposed to do with the undelivered envelope. But a shower was in order first.

Thirty minutes later she felt refreshed, albeit still a little tired from the day's events. She picked up the phone and dialed. There were several rings before she heard the familiar voice on the other end.

"Hi, Tony. Have I got some news for you!" She related a brief synopsis of the missing Linda and finding the body.

"Whew, I can't believe it," was his response. "What did you do with the package?"

"Nothing. I still have it. I wanted to get some instruction from you."

"Good. Just hang on to it. I'm going to have to come down there and take care of it myself."

"When will you be here?" Julia was happy to hear that he would be still be coming.

"I'm not sure yet. I'll have to tie up some loose ends up here first. You just put those papers in a safe place for me until I get there. Can you manage until about Wednesday?" Tony asked.

"Of course, but I do miss you." Julia tried her best seductive voice.

"I miss you, too, Babe. I'll call as soon as I have definite reservations. In the meantime, enjoy yourself, but do stay out of trouble, please."

Julia heard him chuckle on the other end. "Of course. Don't worry. I feel better now that I've talked to you. I'll look forward to seeing you Wednesday."

"Right. And maybe you should stay out of caves, too."

"Don't worry! I'll just enjoy the sun for the next few days. Miss you! Bye!"

It was easy to decide what to wear to dinner. She chose a teal blue sundress with a bare back and halter-style crisscross straps. It complimented her tan, that was already golden brown. It was fun to choose clothes that she didn't have to hide under the white coats she wore every day at work in the medical clinic. She suddenly realized

31

how hungry she was. She hadn't eaten since breakfast with Ian. She checked to be sure all was secure and went downstairs to meet Ian.

Ian was a little late. Julia sipped on her wine while enjoying the music of the steel drum band. She sensed Ian's presence before he tapped her on the shoulder. He was flashing the handsome smile that Julia was beginning to like a lot. He sobered quickly and sat down next to her.

"I understand you've had a heck of a day," he said.

"How did you learn that already?" Julia asked, surprised.

"It's all over the island. News like that travels like a prairie fire in August. What made you decide to go looking for Linda in that cave?"

Julia sighed, then said, "Well, she still wasn't home when I checked this morning and I was getting worried. Jill said she thought she knew where the cave was. But I really didn't expect to find anything. Certainly not her body."

"That must have been a pretty big shock," Ian offered in a consoling voice. "Could you tell what had happened?"

"Not for sure. I'm going to ask her parents for permission to do an autopsy."

"That could be hard on them. She probably just pushed herself too hard. After all, she had already been diving earlier that day."

"But we don't know when she died yet. Martin said she called late Friday, so she might have dived Saturday, and that would have been a long enough wait."

"Well, I still don't think an autopsy is necessary," Ian offered.

"Her parents may refuse, but it doesn't hurt to ask." Julia couldn't understand why no one else seemed to want to do the autopsy. Didn't they want to know the actual cause of death? "Anyway, I'm hungry. Let's eat!"

After dinner, Ian escorted Julia to the main lobby and then excused himself for the evening. "Business," he said.

Julia needed some fresh air. She remembered that the Gradys, whom she'd met earlier, had said they'd be at Maho Reef tonight for the hotel cocktail party. Julia decided to join them.

The two hotels were close enough together for walking, so Julia decided to enjoy the night air. Once inside the other hotel, she spotted Jack and Helen right away. Jack waved at her and indicated a place he'd saved. She'd met the Gradys the day before in the restaurant while waiting for Ian to make a phone call. Jack and Helen were a pleasant middle-aged couple from St. Louis. This was their first trip to St. Maarten and they were armed with guidebooks, cameras, suntan lotion and sunglasses when Julia first met them. When they found out Julia was alone, they had invited her to feel free to accompany them any time she wanted company. They exchanged 'hellos' as Julia slid into the empty chair next to Jack.

"Hey, glad you decided to join us. How's your day been? Did you get lots of sun?" Then Jack noticed the stricken look on her face and asked, "What's the matter?"

Julia gave a brief synopsis. Helen commented that she sure wouldn't go diving again after an experience like that.

Julia smiled. "Well, it's one of those things. I'm not afraid to dive, but I will certainly be very careful and won't dive alone!"

"Good!" Jack and Helen chimed. The steel drum band began playing again. Julia was amazed at the beautiful sounds that emanated from the funny-looking instruments. She learned that they were made from the cut-off ends of steel drums, which had been hammered into dishpan shapes. The drums had originally been used to store oil, and were ubiquitous on the island.

She scanned the audience. Some of the faces were familiar. She'd seen them shopping or at the hotel, perhaps. One face particularly stood out. She excused herself for a minute and walked across the room.

"Scott, I'm not sure you remember me, but I came into your shop looking for Linda Townsend yesterday. And I left a message for her."

"Sure, I remember. You wanted to do some diving this week. What can I do for you?" He smiled at her, expectantly.

"Did Linda come in to pick up that message I left?"

"I didn't see her come in, but it was gone today when I glanced at the bulletin board. I just assumed she'd taken it. Why?"

"I finally found her today, but she was dead."

"Dead? Where?" Scott seemed surprised.

"In a cave on St. Bart's."

"You're kidding."

"No, I wish I were. What do you know about Linda?" Julia asked.

"Linda pretty much kept to herself. She spent a lot of time with that silly fish project of hers. I guess she was gathering material for a thesis or something."

"Do you know if she'd had any trouble with her equipment recently?"

"No. She wasn't due for a tank check yet. I'm sure she would have said something if she'd had a problem."

"Did she get her air from you?"

"Not always. There are a couple of other shops with compressors, so she sometimes got air elsewhere."

"What about Friday?"

"I only filled one set of her tanks. She always kept a second set ready to go, but she said she'd taken care of it."

"And you're sure everything was okay with those tanks." Julia wanted to follow through on this line of thinking.

"As far as I could tell."

"And that was Friday?"

Scott thought for a moment. "Actually, I filled it late Thursday because she needed it early Friday morning."

"Okay, well, thanks, Scott. If I think of anything else, I'll come by and talk to you at the dive shop." Julia smiled and returned to the Gradys' table. As Julia rejoined the Gradys, Jack noticed the frown on her face. "What's wrong, Julia?"

"I'm not sure, but I want to know who else saw Linda the past few days. Did you happen to know who the girl was that I'm talking about?"

"Sure, we met her last week when we were going to do some snorkeling. In fact, we saw her—when was it—Thursday night, I think, over at Caravanserai. She was arguing with some British guy; at least he had a British accent," Jack explained.

"Would you recognize him if you saw him again?"

"Yes, I think so. He was quite ordinary looking. Nothing special."

"Did you hear what they were arguing about?" Julia was very curious about this sighting.

"No, I couldn't hear them clearly. It seemed to be over a schedule, or time, or something like that. She finally just got up and left."

Helen nodded in affirmation of Jack's reply.

"Did he follow her?"

"No, he went over to another table for a while, and left about ten minutes later."

"Did you see her after that?"

"I don't remember seeing her again." He turned to his wife. "Do you, Helen?"

"No. Earlier in the week she was talking to that dark-haired man at the dive shop, but I thought he was just a customer there. I heard them talk about doing some diving."

"What dark-haired man?" Julia asked. Her tendency to play detective was in full gear.

"I only saw him once over at the dive shop but like I said, I thought he was just a tourist."

"I'm beginning to think that you don't see this as just an accident," Helen volunteered.

"Let's say that I'm not ruling out any possibilities just yet."

Jack commented, "Surely the authorities will be checking all this out."

"Mr. Thompson seems pretty sure it's just an accident. I'm going to try to get her family to do an autopsy. Maybe we'll learn something new." Julia glanced at her watch and noticed the time.

"Well, I'm about ready to turn into a pumpkin, so I'm going to call it a night. Thanks for the drink, Jack. I'll probably see you two tomorrow."

"Good night, Julia," Jack and Helen said together and smiled as Julia rose from the chair and turned to leave. Julia didn't even notice Ian across the room, talking to a dark-haired gentleman in the far corner as she left.

· · ·

Julia spotted the disarray in her room right away because of having left her night light on. Someone had ransacked the room, looking for what? She didn't have anything valuable with her. Tony's papers were all she could think of. She checked her hiding place and found them to be still there.

Now she was really curious. Why was someone interested in anything in her room? Was it the papers? She decided to look at them and broke the seal on the outside envelope. She was disappointed, yet intrigued to find that there was nothing but several sheets of paper with some strange words and numbers. It appeared to be written in some kind of code. Julia shrugged her shoulders as she thought about everything that had happened so far. This was getting more, instead of less, confusing. She decided not to tell Tony about opening the envelope just yet. After securing the envelope again, she got ready for bed. She definitely needed to know more about Linda. She decided to start by asking Jill in the morning.

CHAPTER FIVE

Doing the Limbo

After a somewhat restless night, Julia awoke to the alarm's buzz and jumped out of bed. She was anxious to talk to Jill so she hurried through her morning routine. A few minutes later she was outside at the designated meeting place.

Jill was also on time. Julia spotted her coming down the road towards the hotel and ran out to meet her.

"Good morning, Jill. How was your night?" she asked cheerfully.

"I didn't sleep well. How about you?"

"Same here. I want to ask you about Linda. How well did you know her?"

"About as well as anybody did, I suppose. We used to work together at Underwater Sports when she first came to St. Maarten."

"How long ago was that?"

"She's been here about two years, I guess."

"Do you know where she came from and why she came here?"

"She's from the states. Boston area, I think. She'd gone through a divorce and wanted a complete change, from what she told me."

"Do you know any of her friends, or the people she hung around with?"

"Well, she really spent a lot of time diving and working on her fish. And she did quite a bit of diving for Ian."

"Ian McDonnell? Why? What did he need diving for?" Julia was curious, again.

"They were a real hot item when she first moved here. Everyone thought they'd get engaged and married, but they seemed to fight a lot. Eventually she started just working for him instead of dating him. They got along better that way," Jill said, smiling.

"Why does Ian need someone diving in his business?"

"He has a side business doing recovery work. I think it's his real love, if you want my opinion."

"Next subject. What do you know about Martin Thompson?" Julia was in full detective mode.

"Linda seemed to be mostly just a friend to him. I don't think he was really her type. He was too serious and he was really tied up with his work with the government."

"Hmmm. I don't understand why a British person would be in government on a Dutch and French island," Julia commented, puzzled.

Jill laughed. "He's been here longer than almost anyone I know, except the natives. Fourteen years or so. I've never really thought about his being British. But I guess it is a bit unusual."

"Did Linda have any other boyfriends?"

"She talked about some other guys, but I don't recall meeting any particular ones. She was still pretty broken up about Ian, although she would never let him know."

"Did she dive alone very often?"

"Most of the time. She was good and didn't take chances. That's what's so surprising about her being dead. It shouldn't have happened to her." Jill's voice started breaking up with that comment.

They ran in silence for awhile. Jill pointed out some of the local landmarks as they covered their three miles. Julia recognized a few places such as the airport, the road to Linda's house and the night club where she'd been the night before.

Jill finally spoke up. "You seem really interested in Linda. Is there a reason?"

"It's most likely just a coincidence, but I was supposed to meet her for my friend at home, and it just seems ironic that this should happen. I just can't make the connection, but Tony will be here in a couple of days and I can ask him then."

"So, I'll get to meet this mysterious Tony," Jill grinned.

"Yes. You'll like him. But he's already taken!"

They neared the hotel and the two women slowed down to a walk to cool down. Jill spoke next. "What are your plans for today, Julia?"

"I think I'll take that sailing trip I planned over to St. Bart's and start enjoying this vacation. It hasn't been fun yet. Do you have any plans for tonight?"

"Nothing special. Do you?"

"The Gradys invited me to join them. You're welcome, too. They planned to go to one of the hotel cocktail parties. It would be fun to have one more person."

Jill thought for a second before replying, "Thanks, I think I'd like that. What time are you meeting?"

"Seven o'clock at the hotel lounge."

"Okay, I'll be there. Have a fun day, Julia. Ciao!"

"Ditto."

They both waved as Jill ran off and Julia turned to enter the lobby. Julia glanced at her watch. She had an hour to get ready for the sail to St. Bart's. She was looking forward to a day of sun, and hopefully some fun, too. She hopped into the lobby. She failed to notice the man on the far side watching her.

• • •

The sun was shining warmly as Julia, Jack and Helen climbed aboard the huge catamaran for the two-hour sail to St. Barthelemy, or St. Bart's, as the locals called it. Julia was trying out a new one-piece suit which was turquoise and white stripes with a deep V-neck plunge and high cut legs. There were about 25 people on the boat with a crew of three: two men and one woman, who seemed to be as strong as the men when it came to handling the sheets (ropes on a sailboat).

The tourists were male and female, old and young, tanned and pale, big and small. Some looked better in their bikinis and trunks than others.

Julia stationed herself at the front of the catamaran near another couple she'd met earlier. They were from England. Julia learned that he was a solicitor, and then was relieved to find that in England a solicitor is an attorney, not a prostitute. They told her they would be here for three weeks, partly business and partly pleasure. Julia was laughing so hard that her sides ached as she listened to Frank and Pauline describe their adventures in their rental car. Frank was having trouble adjusting to driving on the right-hand side of the road, which was compounded by having the gear box on the wrong side of his knee.

The sail to St. Bart's was refreshing in the warm air. There was just enough breeze to be comfortable and enough sun to need sunscreen. After a gin and tonic at the open bar, Julia clambered back to the center of the boat to talk with Jack and Helen.

"Julia, is there enough sun for you today?" quipped Jack.

"Almost! It'll do for now, anyway. What did the captain say about touring the island? I was visiting with a British couple and didn't catch his instructions."

"Well, he seems to think that a guy named 'Valentine' is a good tour driver. There'll be a bunch of men waiting with mini-busses and taxis when we get to the dock. They'll give us a guided tour of the island, then take us to a place for lunch, then back to the town for shopping before it's time to leave to go back," Jack explained.

"Jill said the best place to eat is 'Chez Francine'," Julia offered.

"That's one of the places recommended in my guidebook, too. That's probably a good choice if the locals eat there. We can always ask our guide, too. If you get off the boat before us, see if you can nail Valentine for us."

"Will do," Julia replied as she arose to return to her spot in the sun.

As she scrambled back to the bow, Julia noticed that several of the passengers looked rather pale, and were obviously seasick. This was not a fun cruise for all, apparently. She rejoined the British couple and enjoyed the remainder of the sail to St. Bart's. She was able to pick out the white sandy beach that would later turn out to be where the restaurant was located. The magnificent catamaran finally pulled into a quaint sheltered harbor.

It was a mad dash to the line of men waiting to be guides, all of them with wide smiles, brown arms, and one with a t-shirt that said 'Valentine.'

Julia was a little disappointed that someone else spotted him first and his friends filled his bus. But the pleasant gentleman next to him offered his bus. "A brand new one," he explained, and Julia gratefully accepted. The Gradys, the British couple (Mr. and Mrs. Howell) and Julia climbed in. The buses were crammed into the parking area so tightly that it was amazing there were no major dents in any of the vehicles, as they moved forward and backward inches at a time to turn around.

Finally, they were on their way. Julia was in front with the driver. "Constant Gumps," he informed them. He also had a car rental business on the island with the 30 or so cars that Julia had seen on her first trip here.

He was of French descent, very rotund, and very proud of his country. There was no poverty on the island. Everybody had a job, mostly dealing with tourism.

The island tour was a series of going up and down hills on narrow roads with steep grades. It seemed they were looking at water again every few minutes as the road wound around the hills.

Constant pointed out the many homes of the "rich Americans," as he put it. Everything was so picturesque that Julia asked him to stop frequently for a picture of this hillside and that rock fence, and even a beautiful cemetery. The French and the Swedish were buried in separate cemeteries, much to everyone's surprise.

Constant pointed out the different things that most tourists liked to see. Julia was practicing her rusty high school French and Constant was delighted to oblige with correct French words whenever she drew a blank.

All too soon they pulled onto the shoulder of the narrow road behind some tired-looking buildings. "Chez Francine," Constant announced.

It certainly didn't look like much, thought Julia, but the smell of the food being prepared was wonderful. The five friends found a table near the beach. All there was to the cafe was a small enclosed kitchen and an open terrace for dining, with a cover of thatching. They could almost touch the beach from the table.

After a delicious meal of grilled chicken and grilled fish, and lots of tropical fruits, Jack, Helen and Julia strolled down the beach. Jack was a little surprised, yet delighted to find a topless bather on the beach, and disappointed to have a dead battery in his camera. Much to his dismay, she was dressed by the time he reloaded with a freshly charged one.

They continued for another few minutes and discovered that the airport was nearby. The landing strip literally ended at the beach. Julia recalled seeing it earlier with Ian from the other end.

Julia enjoyed wading in the warm water as the sun caressed her body. All too soon, it was time to meet Constant for the drive to town for some shopping. She resolved to return to the beach later.

Only a few minutes later, they were downtown. Julia went off by herself to explore the many little boutiques. She found a few things to take back to her family. She was making her way back to the dock when she saw a familiar silhouette further up the street. She almost called out to him, but stopped when she saw that he was busy talking to someone who was out of her line of vision. She glanced at her watch, shrugged her shoulders and hurried to the dock to re-board the catamaran. The captain had said he sailed promptly at 3:30 PM and wouldn't bother with a head count. Julia wasn't taking any chances.

Once back at the hotel after the return sail, Julia first checked for messages, but there were none. Julia took her time getting ready for dinner. The sun was successfully turning her skin dark brown very quickly, thanks to her Scandinavian genes. She had a bit of a hard time deciding what to wear, but finally settled on a 2-piece outfit in a muted burgundy print. It was the latest style with a short split-skirt, that looked good with Julia's long legs. She secured Tony's papers and then left to join Jill and the Gradys. She was looking forward to an evening of trying the local night life.

The steel drum band was providing excellent background music for the group of young people dancing at 'Studio 7.' Jack spotted an empty table near the dance floor. Julia knew she'd never seen such wonderful dancing anywhere! She was amazed that the band members got such beautiful music out of the funny-looking steel drums.

She danced most of the dances. The locals seemed to enjoy dancing with the tourists and ensuring a good evening of fun. And they were good dancers. It took a few minutes to catch on to the calypso beat and she wasn't used to the dance steps, but before long she was enjoying the intricate local dance patterns. She thought of Tony briefly, and of John back home, then found herself dancing again with still another excellent dancer.

The entertainment of the night was a young, lithe limbo dancer. She twirled and swayed and shuddered as she slithered under the bar—-first at 3 feet, then 2-1/2 feet and 1-1/2 feet. When the bar was lowered to one foot, Julia was sure the dancer couldn't possibly squeeze under the bar. Even her knees were higher than that! But Madame Sophie did! After rousing applause from the audience, she asked for volunteers from the audience.

Julia found herself being helped to the front as a "volunteer" with Jack and Helen encouraging her. There would be a bottle of Champagne for the winner, Madame Sophie announced. There were several young women and a couple of men standing somewhat nervously as Julia joined them.

Julia was glad she'd already had several glasses of wine. She watched as the first contestants made a pass at the limbo bar. The crowd cheered as each successfully cleared the 4-foot level. It was now her turn. She made her first pass—voila! Next turn, she was ecstatic as she cleared the bar at 3 feet. Her earlier ballet training was paying off after all. The 2-1/2 floor level was a bit trickier. Madame Sophie was providing some encouragement as Julia tried to balance herself with her legs spread wide apart. She moved her feet slowly as she inch-walked under. Success again!

The other "volunteers" all made it as well, some more gracefully than others. Okay, this was it—2 feet. Or was it 1-1/2? No matter. It felt like 6 inches as Julia got her body even lower. Balance was more difficult. She felt Madame Sophie's knees under her back for support as she inched forward and cleared again! The audience was cheering as she stood up.

Now to choose the winner. Madam Sophie announced, "Okay, the audience chooses the winner. I give all the participants a number, and when I call this number, you must applaud for the winner. Whoever gets the most applause wins the bottle of Champagne. Understand?" The crowd cheered their reply.

"Okay, who thinks number one is the winner?" Everybody cheered, including Julia. Number one was a short, chunky dark girl who could almost walk under the bar—not fair!

Madame Sophie was asking for applause for number 2. More cheering. Number 2 was a tall dark male. He'd definitely done the low limbo bar once or twice before. There were a few boos from his crowd of friends. Julia was number 3. The band added its sentiments with drum roll. Julia couldn't believe the noise! Then number 4 was being cheered—-another short girl who had fallen when she came through the third time. But that didn't seem to matter. The cheering continued as number 5 bowed. He had bright red pants on and seemed a bit stiff. He had quit after the second pass, but he got his reward for effort.

Julia was caught up in the excitement as Madame Sophie announced, "Number 3 is the winner!" Julia blushed profusely as she accepted her champagne and rejoined Jack and Helen and Jill. They congratulated her and toasted her accomplishment. The whole crowd joined in the victory celebration as champagne flowed freely, on the house! Jack apologized for not having a camera handy. After all, it wasn't every day that one won a limbo contest!

Julia was catching her breath between dances when she spotted the best-looking guy in the room. He was sitting with a blond woman about 20 feet away. They seemed to be arguing. Julia couldn't decide whether he was native to the country or maybe Spanish, or maybe from the Mediterranean. The dark moustache disguised his age, but not his handsome features.

She thought of John back home for a fleeting moment, but stifled her pangs of guilt immediately. This is vacation, she reminded herself, and he had told her to have a good time. She suddenly realized that the handsome gentleman was looking right at her with a broad smile. She'd been caught daydreaming again. She smiled back and returned his wave. The blond woman seemed to have disappeared. To the powder room; perhaps? Julia was pleasantly surprised when he picked up his glass and came toward her table.

"May I join you, Miss Number Three?" he grinned profusely. He was shorter than he'd seemed at first, but tall enough. Julia always felt little awkward around men who were shorter than 5'10" because she was 5'6" herself and liked to wear three-inch heels. He was about 5'11" with a dark tan, dark brown hair, and dark eyes, in addition to a full moustache. Julia invited him to sit down, suddenly a little flustered. He had a slight accent—-British perhaps? Yet he didn't look British.

Julia spoke. "You caught me daydreaming. I was wondering if my friends would believe me winning that contest without pictures to prove it," Julia finally managed to say.

"Oh, so you are not with your friends?"

"Yes and no. I came here to the islands alone, but met some people after I arrived. They're out dancing over there." She pointed toward the Gradys. "The older couple over there." And Jill is dancing out there somewhere as well."

He interrupted, "And home is where?"

"Washington, state, that is. Do you know where that is?"

He smiled, "Why, of course! I have been to your country many times. And what brings you to our 'Friendly Island?' Is this a pleasure holiday?"

Julia noticed that Europeans used the term "holiday" instead of vacation.

"All pleasure. Well, almost all." She didn't elaborate.

He extended his hand. "Perhaps I should introduce myself. I am Greg Plummer and you are…"

"Julia Fairchild. Nice to meet you." Julia took has hand and blushed.

"Can I buy you a drink?" he asked.

Julia frowned, "What about the blond you were with a few moments ago?"

"No problem. We were only making plans for a scuba trip on Tuesday. She works here on the island and has a friend with a boat that I would like to use for a few days. This was a good place to meet. She is frequently here in the evenings."

Julia was relieved, having felt slightly envious without any real reason. Julia introduced Jack and Helen as they rejoined her, laughing as they left the dance floor. It seemed that Helen's zigging wasn't matching Jack's zagging, and they'd collided with another couple on the dance floor. Jill was still dancing.

After a few minutes of visiting, Greg volunteered to escort Julia home and watch for her safety. Julia accepted the offer and the handsome couple left with Jack and Helen swaying to the gentle Calypso beat of the band.

The night air was very comfortable. Just a tiny breeze was rustling the leaves as Greg and Julia walked to the car. Another Mercedes!

"I should have known you'd drive a beautiful car. What kind of work do you do?"

Greg seemed to wince a little, "I'm an importer. You notice our many duty-free shops here? I supply many of them with their merchandise. Business is growing rapidly on this island as tourism increases yearly. It's not quite high tourist season now, but in a few more weeks, there will be many more people here. And my business will be very happy. I make the tourists happy, and they make me happy. Everyone should be happy, no?"

Julia laughed. Everyone did seem pretty happy here, no matter what their job was. Even the taxi driver who met her that first night had told her that St. Maarten was the Friendly Island, and that everybody should be happy on vacation.

Greg turned the car into a beautiful park-like parking area and stopped the car near the entrance. Julia was impressed as the doorman greeted Greg by name and wondered if he escorted different women every night. Probably that type, she thought to herself.

They entered the casino upstairs and approached the roulette table on the far side. It was very crowded because it was after 10:00 P.M. It was also very lively. The island seemed to wake up at 10:00 P.M. and go back to sleep at 4:00 or 5:00 A.M. Since Julia was still experiencing a little lag from the time zone difference, she didn't feel quite so lively, but all the new experiences kept her interested. She shook off the yawn that tried to escape as Greg guided her around the corner, where Julia recognized Martin standing with some other people.

"Greg! What a surprise! We didn't expect to see you until tomorrow." Martin was talking to several people near the door.

"Julia, I'd like to introduce you to Martin Thompson. He is one of the local imports. He and I are among the long-term residents. Martin, meet Julia Fairchild, from Washington. State, that is." He emphasized that, as Julia had. "I happened to be lucky enough to make her acquaintance quite by accident at Caravanserai. You should see how she does the Limbo already!" Greg bowed as he said the last.

Julia blushed again. That was one of her trademarks. The more she tried to control it, the worse it got. "We've met." she stated quite simply.

Greg was surprised. "You have?"

"Yes, but it's a long story. And I don't feel like explaining it right now."

Martin added, "I share her sentiments. It's nice to see you again, Julia, and Greg. I'll talk to you tomorrow, Greg."

"Sure, Good night."

Julia and Greg walked back across the room. Julia was clearly distressed.

"What's the problem? You look like you're ready to cry," Greg asked. They sat down near the bar and ordered some drinks.

Julia cleared her throat before speaking, "I met Martin because of an accident yesterday."

"What accident?"

"A girl named Linda Townsend was found dead yesterday in a diving accident."

"Linda? You must be kidding. She's been diving for years." Greg was clearly surprised.

"That's what everybody else says, but Jill and I found her dead."

"Where?"

"In her fish cave."

"I don't believe it."

"Frankly, I don't either and I was there!"

"What do you mean? Do you mean that you were there when she died?"

"No, just that we found her. That's why it bothers me so much." Julia was bordering on tears at this point. "I'm sorry. Let's talk about something else, okay?"

Greg handed her his handkerchief.

"Greg, I don't think I'm going to be very good company for a while. Do you mind if I call it a night and let you take me home?"

"I'd be glad to give you a rain check for the rest of the night," Greg smiled.

They left the casino and drove back in silence. Julia was not thinking about Linda, however. She was powerfully attracted to the handsome man in her company and wanted to see him again. She finally said something as they left the car to enter the hotel. "Thanks for the drink and shoulder to cry on. I really enjoyed your company."

"You are very welcome. I hope I didn't ruin your evening. Martin…"

Julia interrupted, "It's not your fault. You couldn't have known and I shouldn't have let it bother me."

"Perhaps I can make it up to you. How about dinner tomorrow night?"

Julia smiled, "That would be wonderful."

"Great! I'll make some reservations. Is 8:00 okay?"

"Perfect," Julia replied. In more ways than one, she thought to herself.

"All right, 8:00 at your hotel. Thanks, Julia." He planted a gentle kiss on Julia's nose.

"Good night, Greg." Julia floated back into the lounge, where Jill was visiting with Helen and Jack.

Julia was so engrossed in her thoughts that she almost didn't hear Jill ask her about Greg. She finally realized that Jill was talking to her. She told them that they'd met Martin at the casino.

"And, Greg knew Linda."

Jill smiled. "Of course. Greg knows everybody."

"Why?"

"He's just that kind of person," Jill commented as she shrugged her shoulders.

"Okay. So, tell me why you're waiting here for me like vultures, or maybe like my mother."

Jill spoke first. "I just talked to Scott. He said Linda's equipment all checked out. He couldn't find anything wrong with the valves or tanks. So, it's looking more and more like it must have been diver error."

"Is he sure?"

"He said he double-checked, at Martin's insistence."

Julia thought for a moment. "If it wasn't equipment, then maybe Linda did have some kind of a medical problem. When did Martin say her parents are due in?"

"Tuesday morning."

51

"That's tomorrow. We can find out what flight in the morning from Martin, I'll bet. I've got to convince them to do an autopsy." Julia's face showed sheer determination.

"But what will that prove?" Jack finally spoke up.

"I'm not sure, Jack, but I know we're not going to get any answers without it."

She turned to Jill, "Jill, are you running in the morning?"

"You bet. Regular time. How about you?"

"Yes, I'll meet you. Jack, you should join us, too!" Julia grinned as she turned back toward Jack.

"No thanks, my bones are too old for that sort of thing. You young people can run for me."

"Okay. Well, I'm beat. I'm heading for bed. See you all tomorrow." Julia excused herself.

Julia wandered up to her room. She had so many questions without answers. How did Linda die? Was it an accident or not? Who would have a reason to kill her? Who took the note left for her at the shop? What does Tony have to do with all this? Why doesn't Martin want an autopsy? Her train of thought was broken when she noticed that her phone was ringing as she fumbled with the key in the lock. It had rung at least four times before she managed to get the door open. She noticed immediately that her night light was off, but that was her last thought before she felt a thump on her head and fell to the floor.

It was at least several minutes later before Julia sat up and tried to open her eyes. Her head hurt where she'd been struck, right above her right ear. She tried to recall what had happened. All she could remember was that the phone had been ringing and the night light had been off. The phone was now quiet. She plugged in the night light and felt her head. She was in for a goose egg this time for sure. This was getting more bizarre all the time. She had the presence of mind to check for Tony's papers. This time, whoever ransacked the room had been more thorough. Julia knew they were gone before she removed the filter panel. Her fears were confirmed.

She felt a sense of despair and frustration. This wasn't exactly the kind of vacation she had planned. The first thing she had to do was call Tony—-after all; they were his papers. She dialed his number at home. Ten rings and no answer. Nor was there an answer at his office.

Who was responsible? She mentally listed all the people she'd met in connection with Linda and failed to come up with any decent explanations. And what did Tony's papers have to do with all this?

She called Jack and Helen's room. She briefly explained what had happened. She gratefully accepted their invitation to sleep in their room that night. It never occurred to her to report the incident to anyone official, however.

CHAPTER SIX

Then There Were Two

The alarm went off at 6:15 A.M. Julia was already awake. There had been one bad dream after another through the night, in addition to the throbbing of her head. She finally stayed awake in self-defense.

She was glad it was time to get up and meet Jill for their morning run. Maybe Jill would tell her it had all been a bad dream. No, it was real! She'd have to face Linda's parents today. But, first things first, she thought as she dressed. Julia found some aspirin for her headache, which helped. She left the room a minute later and ran down the hall to greet the sun outside. Running always invigorated her. She thought about her plans for the day. She hoped to get time to shop after she stopped at the police station. She still hadn't bought any post cards. She smiled as she realized that she'd most likely beat them home anyway. Typical!

Jill was right on time. They exchanged greetings and Julia noticed that Jill looked as tired as Julia felt. There was silence except for the steady beat of their feet for the first half mile. It had rained during the night and the air was slightly cool and very refreshing. Julia's mind kept returning to the cave and Linda.

She broke the silence as she spoke. "Jill, do you remember seeing Linda's boat anywhere?"

"No, but I really wasn't looking. I would think it should have been pretty close by."

"I didn't see any boat. But how else would she get there? I suppose she could have come from the beach, but that wouldn't make sense when it's faster by boat." Julia was thinking out loud.

"She could have driven to the beach. It's not too far from the road right there and it's only a half mile swim around to the cave. She had such a big boat that she might have thought it was too much bother. And maybe she didn't have anyone to crew for her."

"Yeah, that's probably it. I suppose the police will check on a car and all. I can ask Martin when I go over to meet Linda's parents."

There was a moment of silence, and then Julia spoke again. "What a reason to have to come to this beautiful island!" She shook her head.

They jogged in silence again to the turnaround point. Julia spoke first. "What else are you going to do today?"

"I'm helping out with some lessons this morning, then I think I've got some freedom. I think I'll just take it easy. I didn't sleep real well last night. Oh, and I promised Martin I'd stop by his office after lunch."

Julia smiled, "I didn't sleep well either. I haven't had bad dreams like that since I was a kid. Huge sea anemones were gulping down innocent divers. It was like a sci fi movie in Technicolor, even!"

Jill laughed. It was the first light note of the day. "What are you going to do?"

"First, I'm going to join the Gradys for breakfast. Then I'm going to call and ask about Linda's tank, and I want to do some shopping. I promised myself a dress from St. Maarten. And I want to work on my sun tan. And…" she paused, "I still need postcards."

"That sounds like a heavy agenda!"

"Well, if I stay busy I won't miss Tony so much until he gets here." Jill could tell that Julia was missing her boyfriend. "You are going to let me meet him, aren't you? Or is he one of those guys you don't share?"

"Of course, you'll meet him. He's really a wonderful person. I know you'll like him and he'll be glad to meet you so he can see I was in good hands while diving. He made me promise I wouldn't dive for a few days after I told him what happened to Linda. I probably would have reacted the same way myself."

"Most people would."

They were almost back to the hotel when Jill broke the silence again. "Julia, I'll probably see you later at Martin's office."

"Okay." Julia suddenly remembered a question she'd wanted to ask. "Jill, do you know who lives in the yellow-green house near the airport right down the road where we were running the other day?"

"That's where Scott lives. Why?"

"Are you sure you know which house I mean?"

"There's only one green house on that whole road. Everybody always talks about making him paint it a more tolerable color, but nobody ever does anything about it. Why do you ask about that house?"

Julia decided to keep her thought to herself for the moment. "Oh, I'd just noticed it when we were running."

"It's certainly a noticeable house!"

"It certainly is. Well, I'll see you later. Thanks for the run, Jill."

"Bye!" Jill waved as she ran on. Julia headed for the hotel to shower and have breakfast.

Julia's spirits had improved significantly by the time she'd showered and rested. She was nearly out the door when the phone rang. "Hello," she almost held her breath, hoping it was Tony.

"Miss Fairchild, this is Martin Thompson. I know you wished to be informed of Miss Townsend's parents' arrival."

"Yes, when are they due?"

"Approximately 11:30 A.M. I'll meet them myself. Would you like to meet us at my office, say—after lunch. Maybe about 1:30?"

"Yes, that would be fine. By the way, I need to report a break-in to you."

Martin was clearly surprised: "A what?"

56

"A break-in. I'll tell you all about it later." Julia's voice was quite firm.

"Very well. Cheerio, then. We'll see you after lunch."

Julia cradled the receiver slowly. She was rather surprised that Martin had invited her to join him and Linda's parents.

A few minutes later, she joined Jack and Helen in the dining room. The sun shone in the room and bounced off the glass and chrome tables.

Jack and Helen greeted her with smiles. "Are you sure you're feeling okay?" Helen asked.

"Yes, of course. It was just a bump on the head. We women are tougher than that." Julia smiled to reassure Helen.

"Do you have any idea who it was?" Jack broke in.

"No, but it has to have something to do with Linda because they took the papers that I had for her."

"What papers?"

"I suppose I can say something now. I was just asked to deliver some papers to Linda for my friend, Tony."

"And you don't have any idea what it's all about?" Jack was obviously both curious and surprised.

"No, Tony didn't say and of course, Linda didn't say. And I didn't ask Tony before I left. And now I can't get in touch with him." Julia shrugged her shoulders as she finished.

She was still perusing the menu when the waiter arrived to take their orders.

After he left, she went on, "I'll call him today. He should be in the office in the next hour or so. I tried last night but couldn't connect. I even forgot to report the break-in to the hotel last night!"

Jack commented, "We were more concerned about you. We can report it today. Did you learn anymore about Linda's parents?"

"Yes, in fact Martin Thompson just called and invited me to meet them at his office this afternoon. I was rather surprised because he hasn't been too receptive about my wanting an autopsy."

"Maybe he's changed his mind."

"Maybe, but I doubt it. However, he can't claim equipment failure. It appears now to be diver error. Anyway, I'll find out later today. What are your plans today?"

"We thought we'd take the hydrofoil over to Antigua. We hear there are a lot of beaches over there.

Julia teased, "So you're into beaches now? Like the one on St. Bart's with the topless ladies?"

Jack blushed, "We'll be looking for shells, not bikinis. What else do you have to do today, Julia?"

Julia was attacking her English muffin and poached egg hungrily as she answered, "See Martin and buy postcards."

They all laughed and finished breakfast, then headed their separate ways.

• • •

Julia first approached the desk clerk to inquire about reporting the break-in the night before. The manager came over promptly to talk with her.

"I do not believe this. We never have this problem before. Are you sure you were not drinking too much?"

That made Julia a bit angry. "I am quite sure that someone was in my room and hit me on the head and knocked me out. I am not sure why. Perhaps he made a mistake, but Jack and Helen Grady can verify my story."

"Very well, Miss Fairchild. We shall investigate this situation. You do realize it would have been easier if you had reported this last night."

"I apologize. I didn't think about it at the time. It is my fault. I do appreciate anything you can come up with. I'll be out for the midday but you can leave a note in my message box if you learn anything." With that, she exited the lobby.

Julia hopped into her silver Toyota and headed for the dive shop. She wanted to look at those tanks herself. The shop was fairly busy for such an early hour. It was barely 9:30 A.M. Scott wasn't readily available, so she approached a young girl behind the counter. "Excuse me, is Scott working today?"

"Yes, but he's not due in until a little later. Can I help you?"

"Do you know which tanks belonged to Linda Townsend?"

"The girl that died?"

"Her tanks are over here," as she walked to the far corner of the back room and identified the mini-fifties as Linda's. Julia recognized the set by the original sticker Linda had on the tank.

"Do you suppose I could check these tanks?" Julia asked.

"I guess so, as long as you do it here. Scott is all done with his investigation. What are you looking for?", she asked, now curious.

"Nothing in particular. I was just hoping to find a clue to Linda's death."

"Scott said they checked out okay."

"Yes, that's what I'd heard. I'm just trying to check out every angle." Julia smiled as she started looking over the tanks.

"Are you a detective or something?"

"Not really, at least not in this field. I just feel partially responsible and would like an explanation of her death."

The clerk said, "I see," excused herself, and went to help another customer, leaving Julia with the tanks.

Julia wasn't sure what she was looking for, as she checked all the valves and pins and connections for anything out of the ordinary. She wrote down some notes and left after about 15 minutes. A tanned gentleman at the camera counter left the shop right behind her.

Julia had three hours before she had to meet Martin. She had planned to shop, but the sun was so bright and the beach so tempting that she found herself changing into a bikini when she returned to her room. Jill had told her where the best beaches were, so armed with her book, beach towel and sunglasses, she headed to one about a mile from the hotel.

Once there, she found it was not crowded, being occupied by only a handful of people. She settled down for some good reading. She'd found an Agatha Christie murder mystery that she'd never read and was anxious to get into the story.

Thirty minutes later, she was finding the story so interesting that she failed to notice that she'd been joined by anyone until he spoke. "Hello, my pretty Julia."

Julia startled a bit, "Well, hi, Greg. Are you playing hooky from work today?"

"No, I have already done what is necessary for now, and I decided to get some sun, as you're doing. Mind if I join you?"

"Not at all." Julia suddenly felt very warm.

"I noticed your book. What are you reading? I hope it's educational."

"Very!" She laughed. This could be a plot for Agatha Christie here, she thought to herself. Greg was smiling. He was very charming, and, well, gorgeous. He was so dark, he really didn't need any more suntan. Julia was glad she'd already turned pretty brown, and didn't burn first, like a lot of her friends. Greg had a funny look on his face.

"What is that look all about?" Julia asked.

Greg looked a little embarrassed. "I'm afraid I can't reveal my thoughts. They are rather risque'."

Julia was feeling even warmer. She had been thinking rather risque' thoughts herself. She turned over on her back to break the silent mood. Greg had brought some wine and offered her a paper cup. She accepted. It tasted good and cool. The first cupful went down quickly.

"Let me propose a toast. Here's to happiness and sunshine!" Greg said, as he poured second cups and handed one to Julia.

"Ditto," Julia raised her cup and took a sip of wine. She then realized before he did anything that Greg was going to kiss her. He slowly moved his hand across her stomach, circled her breasts, and kissed her, first gently, then with more pressure as Julia relaxed and opened her mouth to response to his probing tongue. Greg's hands were warm and soft as he caressed her bare skin. Julia found herself enjoying his touch. She was ordinarily quite reserved and was surprised at her response to Greg, being almost a stranger. Her pulse quickened as he pressed his body against hers.

"Greg, this is a public beach."

"I know. They've seen much worse here."

"But I'm not used to this."

Greg was trying to unhook her top. Julia was flushed. Her body was saying 'yes,' as her head was saying 'no.' She enjoyed the warmth of the sun and the warmth from inside. The alcohol was helping to loosen her up. Still, she wasn't interested in being exposed on the beach. She reached up to hook the top, but found Greg's hand too strong.

"What's the matter, Julia?"

"Too much wine and sun. I think I better cool off."

"We could cool off at my house," Greg offered, smiling.

"No, Greg, not right now." Julia struggled to pull his hand away, and finally succeeded. "I'm sorry. I guess it was the wine and the sun. I shouldn't have let you kiss me."

"And deny me the pleasure of getting to know you a little better?"

Julia reddened. She was confused because she didn't usually let her sexual side surface at all until she was very comfortable with a man. Somehow, Greg had touched some nerve that seemed to override all her usual inhibitions.

"I'm afraid I must be getting back to the hotel. I have an appointment with Martin."

"About Linda?"

"Yes, to meet her parents."

"Oh, that. Well, I won't hold you up. You do remember about dinner tonight at eight?"

"Oh, Greg, I don't know. Maybe I should take a rain check."

"Sorry, I insist. I will behave like a gentleman. Scout's honor! Deal?" Greg crossed his heart, held up two fingers of his right hand and crossed the fingers on his left.

Julia laughed, "Okay, deal. And no hard feelings about this."

Greg roared, "Deal! I'll pick you up at 7:45 P.M."

• • •

Julia was just finishing getting dressed when the phone rang. It was Jill.

"Hi, Jill, What's up?"

"Remember when you asked me about the ugly green house and I said that Scott lived there?"

"Yes, why?"

"He doesn't live there anymore. They found him dead there a little while ago."

"You're kidding! How? Why? Who?"

"I don't know any more than that. There are no suspects yet, but I thought you'd want to know."

"Thanks, Jill…I'll ask Martin about it when I meet him."

Julia put the receiver down slowly. First Linda, now Scott. Is there only one murder, or two? She was convinced that Linda's death was not accidental, regardless of everyone else's opinion. And Scott couldn't have died accidentally in his own house. She would start at Martin's office and then start asking neighbors of Linda and Scott. There had to be a clue somewhere, if she could only find it.

CHAPTER SEVEN

Missing Puzzle Pieces

Julia hadn't known what to expect when meeting Linda's parents. They were younger than she had anticipated, and they appeared to be fairly wealthy. Martin introduced them to Julia as Mr. and Mrs. Desmond Rooke from Framingham, Massachusetts. Julia nodded and forced a smile. "Pleased to meet you. I suppose you know that my friend Jill and I found Linda in the cave."

"Yes, that's what Mr. Thompson said," Mr. Rooke replied.

"Did he ask you about an autopsy?"

"No, he said it was an accident, so we didn't think an autopsy was necessary," Mr. Rooke responded. Mrs. Rooke nodded in agreement with her husband.

"That may be true, but I disagree about the autopsy. It would show the actual cause of death and could confirm whether it was an accident or not. Especially since there have been two deaths now." Julia paused.

Mrs. Rooke gasped. "Two deaths? We didn't know that. Mr. Thompson, is that true?"

Martin appeared a little flustered. "Yes, but I just learned of the other one myself. And we don't have any evidence of a connection at this point." He turned to Julia, "And just how did you learn about this, Miss Fairchild?"

It was Julia's turn to blush. "It is true, then?"

"Yes, although I don't know any details yet. A young man was found this morning by his neighbor. The police will investigate it, you can be sure."

Mr. Rooke asked, "Julia, do you really think an autopsy would be helpful?"

"I'm not sure, but it couldn't hurt. Everyone agrees that she was an excellent diver so something drastic must have happened to her."

"Okay. I respect your opinion. Mr. Thompson told us you were a physician in the States. Where would an autopsy be done?"

Martin answered, "We have no pathologist here. There would have to be some kind of arrangements made."

Julia quickly volunteered. "I have a friend in Boston who would be able to do it. We could have some preliminary results by Wednesday afternoon or Thursday morning, I'm sure."

"Then that's what we'd like to do. Right, Darling?" Mr. Rooke asked the last of his wife, as she nodded, again in agreement.

Julia couldn't be sure, but she thought Martin looked angry for a moment, but he quickly regained his composure. "Very well, Julia. I will have you make the proper arrangements while I take care of the legal matters with Mr. and Mrs. Rooke."

Mrs. Rooke spoke up, "Thank you, Miss, I mean, Doctor Fairchild. I do hope you can get some answers for us. She's my only daughter. We weren't close, but I did love her."

"I know you did, and you can call me Julia. I'm on vacation from being a doctor this week. I'll make some phone calls and get back to you right away." Julia smiled, and extended her hand, secretly pleased that she had won this round. But for what? She wasn't sure there was any kind of a prize when murder was involved.

Twenty minutes later all the arrangements had been made and the Rookes were gone. Julia was about to leave as well when Martin asked her about the break-in.

"Oh, I almost forgot! It seems like ages ago now."

"But it was last night?" Martin was confirming with Julia.

"Yes, about 10 P.M. I'd just gotten back to my room after drinks with the Gradys. I don't remember anything except that my night light was turned off and my room was a mess. I was hit on the head from behind and didn't come to for 10 or 15 minutes, I guess." Julia rubbed her head as she remembered where she'd been struck.

"Do you have any idea why?"

"Yes and no. He or she stole some papers that I was supposed to give to Linda. They were hidden in my room. They were gone when I came to. But no one knew I had them except Ian and Jill. And they certainly wouldn't have done this!"

"Okay. Any suspects?"

"If I knew what the papers meant, it would be easier to figure out why they were stolen. But I really don't have any idea what they were all about."

"And you say these papers belonged to your friend, Tony. Have you asked him what they were for?"

"His name is Tony Romero, but I haven't been able to reach him for two days. I can't tell him anything until I get through. He's supposed to be here Wednesday, but he hasn't left any definite word on that."

Martin had more questions. "And you don't know why you were to give them to Linda?"

"No, no idea. Oh, I almost forgot—someone also ransacked my room two nights ago, probably looking for the papers, but they didn't find them that night."

"And I suppose you reported that to the authorities," Martin said quite sarcastically.

"You know I didn't. It didn't even occur to me to do that. But I did report it to the hotel manager."

"Perhaps if you had, we could have prevented the second break-in."

"Perhaps. I honestly didn't realize how serious it was. Do you think Scott's death has anything to do with this?"

"I don't see how, Julia." Martin seemed sincere in his response.

66

"Well, Scott knew I was looking for Linda, but that's the only connection I can come up with."

"I assure you, we will investigate thoroughly, Julia."

Julia could tell that the interview was over. "Will you let me know what you find out?"

"Of course," Martin replied with a wry smile.

Julia wasn't so sure, but she left anyway. She'd never expected a vacation with so many complications. She felt a great need to talk to Tony and decided to call him again once she got back to the hotel.

. . .

Julia let the phone ring 15 times before she hung up. She remembered her mother saying that a phone rang ten times per minute, and that it was only decent to give someone at least one minute to answer. With that reasoning, she'd give Tony 1 ½ minutes, and that was more than enough. She tried his office number next and was relieved to hear a voice on the other end. Especially Tony's.

"Hi, Tony. It's Julia. Better sit down for this one."

"What's the matter, Love?"

Julia related the story to him, trying not to leave out anything important. When she finally finished, she was crying. It was the first time she'd realized how scared she was.

Tony tried to calm her down. "Julia, you could be in danger. Do you have any idea who is behind all this?"

"No. None of it seems to fit together right. I was always good at working jigsaw puzzles and crossword puzzles, but this puzzle is a bit harder. Some pieces are missing!"

"Julia, I want you to leave it to the authorities. And be careful until I get there." Tony was firm over the phone.

"When is that?" Julia asked.

"I can't get away until Friday. But stay out of this, do you hear me?"

Julia felt somewhat comforted by his concern. "Yes, I hear you." But she didn't promise to stay out of it.

Julia slowly put the receiver back in the cradle. It was nice to hear his voice. She definitely needed to relax a bit more after today. She went to the kitchenette and opened the mini-fridge. She had an open bottle of Chardonnay that would do for starters. She poured herself a glass of wine and sat down to watch an old movie on an American movie station.

Most of the hotels had satellite dishes for television reception. She had been surprised one evening to be watching WGN-9 in Chicago at a time when she knew John would be there, visiting his mother. The news had said it was snowing in Chicago. It was hard to imagine snow when the island temperature was 80 degrees!

Half a glass of wine later, she still wasn't interested in the movie and decided to change clothes and go downstairs instead. Maybe she'd see somebody she knew—the Gradys might even be available. She quickly dialed their room number, but there was no answer.

She resolved to at least meet one new person, even if it was going to have to be the bartender! She smiled to herself as she tried to imagine herself sitting on a barstool, making jokes with the bartender. She couldn't. She put on a t-shirt dress that was just right for the weather, finished the last swallow of her wine and then stepped out the door.

Julia sat down at the bar and ordered a second glass of Chardonnay. She thought of old James Cagney movies as she surveyed the small crowd in the bar. It was a strange time of day, in a way. At 4:30 P.M., it was too early to get ready for dinner, too late to go to the beach, and too late for shopping. There were a number of other people who seemed to be killing time in the bar, like Julia was. It was a nice place, with open windows letting in a cool breeze, lots of wicker, and various shades of green for the primary color decor. It was very refreshing. And the wine was just what she needed.

Julia was daydreaming about lying on the beach with the sun caressing her body when a familiar voice broke the spell.

"Well, Miss Julia, it seems I have caught you sleeping again!" Ian laughed as he spoke.

Julia smiled. She couldn't resist Ian's handsome smile. "Not sleeping—just daydreaming."

"About what?"

"Sunshine and beaches."

"As I recall, that's how I met you the first time, daydreaming in the sunshine on the beach," Ian smiled broadly.

Julia giggled. Ian was handsome in his trim khaki slacks and light blue and white striped polo shirt. She was sure he knew it, too. But she felt good and was glad she'd chosen the teal blue dress to put on. It showed off her legs and tan.

Ian broke the momentary silence. "Your dress matches your eyes, but it doesn't sparkle like they do. What say we go out for a drive?"

Julia nodded as she finished her wine. She was very attracted to Ian for reasons she didn't want to explain.

Ian appeared to be very relaxed behind the wheel of his Mercedes. The top was open to the sky, so Julia enjoyed the wind and sun on her face.

"Where are we going?" Julia finally asked.

"Somewhere you've never been," he replied, as he pulled up to a beautiful house overlooking the ocean. It was sitting on a hill with no other houses in the immediate view.

"Whose house is this?"

"Mine."

Julia was astonished. She took a deep breath and pinched herself. She hadn't realized that Ian had the kind of money it would take to own such a beautiful piece of property.

"Let me give you a tour," Ian said as he took her by the hand.

Julia let herself be helped from the car and into the house. She couldn't believe her eyes. Everything was tastefully done—simple but comfortable, and quietly expensive. She sipped at yet another glass of Chardonnay as Ian pointed out the origin of various treasures.

When they got to the back patio, Julia wished she'd thought to bring her camera. The view was wonderful. Ian had his arm around her as he explained how he happened to be the owner of this beautiful house. Julia found herself feeling very warm as she listened to his smooth voice. She hardly noticed when he stopped talking and began kissing her instead. She had known he would be a good kisser. She found herself being led to the small pool where the Jacuzzi was swirling away.

They both slipped their sandals off and sat down at the edge of the Jacuzzi. Ian had his arm around Julia as they dangled their feet in the blue water under the warm Caribbean sun. The warm water was like a tonic, even in the late afternoon. Julia felt very relaxed and thought about yachts, sailing and never having to go to work again.

Ian's voice broke through to her thoughts. "This might be a good time to get naked and initiate the Jacuzzi."

Julia doubted it would be the first time the Jacuzzi had been initiated but let herself be caressed a moment longer before she replied. "Maybe for you, but not for me. I've got a dinner date with some friends and need to take care of some loose ends before I go out. What time is it, anyway?"

"About 5:30, I'd say. Why don't you cancel with your friends and have dinner with me instead?"

"Honestly, I would if I knew how to contact them right now, but I did promise—and I do have some business to take care of." Julia smiled sweetly at Ian.

"Well, if you insist, but you owe me a dinner date another night."

"Ian, I promise, but now I should go."

Once back at the hotel, Julia called Jill. She was glad to find her at home. "Jill, can you dive tomorrow?"

"I can get away about 1:00, if that's not too late. What's up?"

"I want to go back down to Linda's cave and check something out. And 1:00 P.M. would be fine."

"Okay. I'll meet you at Bobby's again."

"Great! I'll be there. Thanks a lot, Jill."

Julia used the time in the shower to think about her plans for tomorrow. She wanted to know more about Scott and the circumstances of his death. Jill could fill in some personal details, and she might learn something from his neighbors. Perhaps she could cajole Martin into giving details about his body being found. She needed to go back into the cave. She felt certain she would find missing links to help solve this puzzle. She knew no more about Tony's package now than she did the day he gave it to her, except that it didn't have anything to do with her. Why would Tony be writing in code? She felt a twinge of guilt for not telling him she'd opened the envelope but he hadn't asked, so she really hadn't lied. She also needed to call George Carlton in Boston about the autopsy. George had been in her medical school class and practiced pathology. She hoped he'd have something that would solve the mystery.

She grinned to herself as she thought of the situation she was in. Her childhood heroines had been Nancy Drew and Trixie Belden. They always seemed to stumble into trouble and solve mysteries right and left, but they were only stories. This was real. Even Jane Marple might have trouble with this one. Julia realized she hadn't finished her novel yet, as the thought of Agatha Christie's problem-solving heroine crossed her mind.

A glance at her watch told her she had only 15 minutes to be ready for Greg. She wasn't sure she was emotionally ready for him after the events of the day. She wasn't used to having the attention of so many men, all at once. She found it frustrating to have to listen to her conscience all the time. She slipped on a cool cotton sundress that was just dressy enough for a week night dinner out, brushed her hair, applied some lipstick and headed downstairs to meet Greg.

Greg was just getting off the phone when Julia spotted him in the lobby. He looked very dapper in light gray slacks and a pale blue shirt. He greeted her with a smile and gentle kiss. Julia returned the smile and kiss.

"I know a great place for dinner for two—good food, good atmosphere, and good music."

"I know—your place!" Julia said, somewhat facetiously.

"You're absolutely r-r-r-wrong! I'm a lousy cook, but I do know the chef at the Rusty Pelican. Will that do?" Greg pretended to plead.

"Perfect. I'm hungry. I forgot to get around to lunch today. I was…uh…busy."

"Yes, I remember." He grinned at Julia. She smiled, recalling the moment.

It was only a short drive to the restaurant. This one also had open walls. That appeared to be the norm here. It was quite busy, considering that is was Thursday, and early. Things didn't get going in St. Maarten until 10 P.M., by and large.

The waiter knew Greg by name, and gave them a table near the water, much to Julia's delight.

"Greg, how well did you know Linda?"

He wasn't prepared for that question. "You never give up on her, do you?"

"Not until I know why she died."

"Everyone knows it was an accident!"

Julia protested. "I don't know that. How well did you know her?"

"Okay, I guess it's been about two years since I first met her."

"But she's only been here about a year, Ian said." Julia was puzzled by his answer.

"That's how long she has lived here. She used to come down from the States about once a month before that. Her husband had business here and she usually came with him."

"What kind of business—diving?"

"No. She did dive while she was here, but he didn't participate as far as I know. She was working in that cave of hers most of the time."

"So, what did her husband do?"

"I'm not sure. He pretty much kept to himself. I heard he threw a lot of money around, especially at the casinos, and I gathered he was fairly well off." Greg was perusing the menu as he answered her questions.

"Does he still come down here? I wonder if he continued business after they divorced." And if he killed her, Julie thought to herself.

"I haven't seen him in several months. After the divorce, Linda moved down here and he pretty much stayed away. She did say once that he was still supporting her, but she worked too, so I guess it wasn't enough, or it might have been for only a certain amount of time."

Greg continued after giving their order to the waiter. "What have you learned about the autopsy?"

"Nothing yet. It's too early. I'm going to call tomorrow and see if there are any preliminary findings."

"I don't know what you expect to find," Greg mused.

"I don't know either. So, I guess we'll both be surprised." Julia smiled as Greg looked at her with a frown on his face. She certainly didn't understand everyone's hesitation about learning more about Linda's death. She decided not to wonder for the moment, as she ate her salad.

The stars and moon were bright as Greg walked Julia back to the hotel lobby. She had turned down his invitation to go dancing, or to go to his place. He had seemed a little miffed, but she wanted to get an early start in the morning and didn't feel like wrestling with the inevitable if she allowed herself to spend any more time with him. She promised to call him the next day to soothe his disappointment.

"Julia, please do be careful."

"Of course," she laughed nervously. I'm not doing anything dangerous."

"That's just it. I don't think you know what dangerous is. "

Julia smiled. "Please don't worry. I will be very careful, and I will call you tomorrow. And thanks for caring."

Greg finally kissed her good night and walked back toward his car.

Julia was a little worried as she walked back to her room. Greg had seemed truly concerned for her safety. Did he know something? She hadn't been able to wheedle anything out of him. Maybe he was just the nervous type. She dismissed any more thoughts of Greg and hurriedly got ready for bed. The fresh sheets were cool on her bare skin. She had jumbled thoughts about Tony and Greg and Ian as she drifted off to sleep.

CHAPTER EIGHT

Rhyme Without Reason

For the first time since Julia's arrival in St. Maarten, the sky was cloudy instead of sunny when she bounced out of bed. It didn't dampen her spirits, however, because she knew it would clear up shortly. She'd learned a little about the weather from Jill. If it rained at all, it did so early in the morning and then it would be clear and sunny the rest of the day, at least in this particular season. Julia quickly pulled on her running togs and raced out the door to meet Jill.

"Hello, Julia!" Jill called from 100 yards away.

"Hi, Jill!" Julia called as she ran to meet her halfway. The two young women ran in silence for the first one-half mile or so. Julia always found the first five minutes the hardest and was glad to get it over with. The next 25 minutes were always easier for reasons she couldn't explain.

Jill broke the silence first. "Did you get permission to do the autopsy?"

"Yes, fortunately. But I don't think Martin is happy about it."

"Oh, he probably just doesn't like a woman interfering in his business, not that I think you're interfering."

"I don't think so, Jill. I really think he's afraid of something."

"Like what?"

"I'm not sure yet. Something funny is going on and I intend to find out what it is."

"Julia, you're going to get into trouble. Let the authorities handle it." Jill sounded truly worried.

"But that means Martin, and he's not handling it properly."

"You're just being overly suspicious. Martin's lived here for years and he's always been very honest. He's very highly respected." Jill was very defensive on this point.

"Well, he doesn't like me much, and I must say, it's mutual at the moment. Not to change the subject, but I need to know what you know about Scott."

"He hasn't been here long. Maybe six to eight months. He got a job at the dive shop right away. In fact, I think Linda helped him get it."

"Really? Did they know each other before?" Julia's curiosity was piqued.

"I'm not sure. He was trying to get a job as a diving guide but didn't have enough experience in this area, so Linda was helping him out. I think that's how he ended up at the dive shop. She was kind of a big sister to him."

"Did he have a girlfriend?"

"Not a special one. He seemed really bashful, and I don't think he had a lot of money for dating."

"Do you know how he was killed? Was he shot?"

"From what the neighbor said, he was clubbed. Nobody heard any shots. It didn't look like they meant to kill him. It may have been accidental."

"Clubbing is accidental?"

"Well, you know what I mean. Anyway, there didn't seem to be a motive for murder. Nothing was missing, apparently."

"Jill, how did you find all this out? Martin certainly isn't that talkative."

"My best friend works in Martin's office and she told me. It wasn't classified information, anyway."

Julia was elated. "Jill, that's wonderful! I was going to have to sweet-talk Martin into telling me what he knew, but you've told me basically what I wanted to know already. I didn't want to raise his hackles any more than I already have anyway."

They were approaching the hotel before either of them spoke again.

"Are we still on for diving at 1:00 P.M.?" Julia asked.

"Sure, I'll arrange for tanks and a boat. And meet you at Bobby's."

"Great. See you there."

Julia walked into the hotel. She couldn't explain why she felt so exhilarated except that she thought she might be getting closer to some answers.

Forty-five minutes later, she was cooled down, showered and dressed. It was still too early to try to call George in Boston, so she decided to drive over to town to have breakfast. She'd been so busy she hadn't done some of the things she'd planned to do while on vacation.

Her first day here she had seen a neat little restaurant on Main Street in Phillipsburg that she wanted to try, especially after Jill told her it had great breakfasts. Today was it!

At first, Julia thought the paper on her windshield was a handbill. Just like at home, she thought. A quick glance told her that her car was the only with anything on it. "Interesting," she said to no one in particular. It was a note that had apparently been placed sometime earlier because it was wet from the morning's sprinkle. The message was foreboding.

"Roses are red.
Violets are blue.
Lewiston is dead.
Next could be you."

Julia shuddered. Who was responsible? She wished she knew. Obviously, someone knew her car. She decided to change cars at the rental agency, in addition to asking for a change in rooms at the hotel. This was a small island, so it would be difficult to become anonymous and invisible, but she wasn't about to leave the island because of a threat. She was more determined than ever to get to the bottom of this! As her Finnish grandfather would say, she'd have to show some "Sisu." Not that she wasn't a little frightened, but she'd gone this far and wasn't to be stopped. She looked around the parking lot but didn't see anything unusual. She climbed into her Toyota and went on to have breakfast.

It was 10:00 A.M. before she finished and returned to the hotel. She arranged for a change in rooms (too noisy, she explained in case someone at the front desk was tipping off someone else) and then placed a call to Boston. She'd already learned that phone service to the United States was notoriously bad and was pleasantly surprised to be rewarded with an expeditious connection.

"Dr. Carlton's office." A pleasant female voice answered the phone.

"Hello, this is Dr. Julia Fairchild. May I speak to Dr. Carlton?"

"May I tell him the nature of your business?"

"I'm calling about Linda Townsend. I arranged for the autopsy on the diver from St. Maarten."

"Oh yes! Just one moment. He would like to speak with you." The female voice was more friendly.

"Julia, is that really you?" George's voice was very smooth and familiar.

"Yes. Hi, George! It's been a long time."

"Too long. Six years now, isn't it?"

"Yes, It's hard to believe we've been out of medical school that long. I really appreciate you taking care of this so quickly. Your receptionist told me you were very busy when I called for the favor, but when I explained the situation, she was very gracious about accepting the body."

"I was surprised to get your message, aw well as pleased to be able to help. Especially for a fellow med student! What can you tell me?"

Julia related the story briefly. "What have you found?"

"Nothing except evidence of carbon monoxide poisoning. The color of her lungs was suspicious so I tested the blood as well, and there's no doubt that she died from lack of oxygen. She'd been dead about 24 hours, plus or minus six hours."

"Carbon monoxide? But the tanks checked out okay. Are you sure? Could it possibly have been an air embolus instead?" Julia was surprised at the news.

"Julia, I'm sure about the carbon monoxide. I considered an embolus but couldn't find enough evidence for one. You better check those tanks again. Now where shall I send this report?"

"Oh, yes, I will have the tanks rechecked. Please send one copy to me and one to Martin Thompson in St. Maarten. The address is on the identification tag. Thanks a million, George. I'll let you know about the tanks after they're retested."

"Good idea. I'm glad I could help you out. Don't wait another six years before you call!"

Julia smiled. "Of course. Bye, George."

Julia was very pensive as she ended the call. Threat or no threat, she had some sleuthing to do. She decided to not tell Martin about the report until after her dive with Jill. She sensed that the longer she waited to tell him, the more she could learn on her own.

First things first, she exchanged cars at the rental agency. They didn't ask any questions, for which Julia was relieved. She needed some help to carry out her new plans and decided to ask Ian. She drove over to his office and climbed the stairs to the upper level, where she saw his name on the first door.

She quickly explained who she was to the receptionist and was escorted into his office.

"Julia! To what do I owe this lovely surprise?"

"Hello, Ian. I need some assistance. I was hoping you'd be able to help me."

"What kind of help? I'm always available to a damsel in distress." He smiled that grin again.

Julia explained about the message on her car. She'd told him earlier about the ransacking of her room. She briefly outlined her new ideas.

"You want me to break into Scott's house?" Ian was surprised at what she was asking him to do.

"Well, I just want to get in to check for any clues that the authorities might have missed. I'm just sure his death has something to do with Linda. And I thought you might still have a key to Linda's house, so we could check there, too." Julia was almost pleading.

"I do have a key, but I'm not too keen about going into Linda's house."

"Ian, please! It's really important! There isn't anyone else I can ask to help me with this!"

Ian softened. "Okay, Sparkly Eyes. I'll help you. When do you want to do all this?"

"I think after dark. We'll have to walk a little way to keep the car out of sight. And I'll have to think of some way to see without using a lot of light."

"I can help there. Let me meet you at the hotel at 9:30 P.M. Is that okay?"

"That'll be fine. I'll wear my best sleuthing clothes!" Julia smiled as Ian got up to escort her to the door.

"I'll see you later, my lovely Julia."

Julia fairly flew down the stairs to her car.

There was a message for her at the hotel. "Call Martin Thompson," it said.

She dialed his office and was connected with him quickly.

"Hello, this is Julia Fairchild. I had a message to call."

Martin's voice boomed in her ear. "I wanted to hear about the autopsy." Martin seemed a little irritated over the phone.

"Oh, Martin. The pathologist hasn't gotten to it yet. They had a big job to do and he promised to get it done sometime in the next 24 hours." Julia crossed her fingers as she fibbed. She thought she heard a sigh of relief as Martin listened.

"Very well. Will you let me know as soon as you learn anything?"

"Yes, Martin."

"You are staying out of trouble, are you not?" Martin's voice was very stern.

Julia thought he sounded truly concerned, and answered, more light-hearted than she felt, "Of course. I've done what I can. I'll let your office handle it from here." Her fingers were crossed again, as she wasn't fully convinced yet.

"Thank you, Julia. I'm very flattered by your confidence." He smiled sardonically.

"You're welcome. I'll talk to you later. As soon as I hear from Dr. Carlton."

Julia found she'd been a little nervous as she ended the call. She glanced at her watch and hurried to her room to change for her dive with Jill.

The sun had indeed come out and was brilliant in the sky as Jill and Julia raced across the water to St. Bart's. It was a good 45 minutes before they were anchored and ready to enter the water. Julia went into the water first and waited for Jill to follow almost immediately. They moved gracefully through the water to the now familiar underwater shaft. Julia noticed right away that someone had been in the cave since they'd been there. Whoever had been there had left a small flashlight on the rock shelf. Julia checked it and found that it was broken.

"Julia, what are we looking for?"

"I'm not sure. Something out of the ordinary. Something that doesn't fit here. Something that has to do with Linda, or maybe Scott. Or someone I don't even know." They looked in all the nooks and crannies for such a something. Jill was the first to finally make a find.

"Julia, look at this." She held up a small plastic bag with some paper in it. "I found this back in that shallow hole in the wall we saw last time."

Julia looked it over. It didn't seem very interesting, but she'd reserve judgment for later. As she looked toward the hole Jill was talking about, a flash of something bright caught her eye. She swam toward the ledge and picked up a small piece of metal. She looked at it more closely and then tucked it into her waist wallet with the plastic bag.

A few more minutes of searching turned up nothing more. The two women decided to head back to the boat and slipped back into the water for the silent trip through the clear blue water.

Julia left Jill at the marina. Her next order of business now was to check out Linda's tanks at the dive shop again. The young man who had helped her earlier when Scott was gone was there again. He allowed her to look over the records of tank fillings. Julia wrote down a few notes and then asked to see Linda's tanks. She was disappointed to learn that they had been confiscated by Martin Thompson the day before. Not that it would stop her from finding out what she wanted to know.

She thanked Steve, as he'd introduced himself, and headed for the hotel again, now to change back into dry clothes. It was still very bright when she left the hotel to go to Martin's office. He hadn't been there when she tried calling him a few minutes earlier. All the better, she thought to herself.

Tony wasn't in either, so she couldn't relate her new findings to him. She did manage to contact the Gradys and arrange to meet them in an hour at the hotel.

She was so deep in thought that she didn't notice the white Mercedes across the lot pull out a few seconds later.

. . .

Martin's secretary was arguing on the phone when Julia stepped into his office. The conversation was in French, so Julia was only able to catch a few words of it. She did understand "car" and "dead," however. She wished she'd polished up her French before this trip. The red-headed woman slammed down the receiver and apologized as she realized Julia had overheard part of what she'd said.

"I don't speak French, so it was all Greek to me," Julia quickly offered. "I would like to see Mr. Thompson, if I may. It's very important."

"I am sorry. He is not in. He had some business in Marigot."

"That's all right. Could I just check on top of his desk? I think I left something there yesterday."

"Oui. Go ahead. I'm sure he won't mind." The red-headed secretary waved her toward his office, somewhat distractedly.

Julia stepped into his office and closed the door. She hoped he'd left the information she needed on his desk. She searched his desk quickly, but didn't find what she wanted. But she did find a set of keys with Scott's address on the tag. These will be useful, she thought to herself. She turned to leave the room when she spotted the bright yellow mini-50 tanks in the corner behind the door. A cursory inspection confirmed that they were the tanks she'd been looking for. She took some more notes and left the office, thanking his secretary as she closed the door behind her.

She hurried down to the car and tried to sort out in her mind all the information that she had. She still didn't have enough to prove anything, but felt she knew where to find the rest.

CHAPTER NINE

A Sneak Peak

Ian made several phone calls after Julia left his office. He had never met anyone quite like her. She appeared to be delicate and fragile, as do many beautiful women, but had a fortitude that would shame most men! She hadn't confided all her knowledge to him, he knew, and he felt certain she was on to something. How much she would uncover remained to be seen. It was curious to him that she trusted him as much as she appeared to. If she only knew, he thought, as he smiled to himself. It looked like he was going to have to make some arrangements for tonight if she intended to go through with her detective playing.

He picked up the phone and dialed a number he hadn't used much recently. When the raspy voice answered, he related what Julia had told him so far. He didn't mention the plans for the evening; that could be relayed later, after they found, or didn't find, whatever she was looking for.

"Okay, Ian. Thanks for the call. We'll get right on it. Do be careful and let's hope your lady friend isn't in over her head."

"Thanks. I'll keep an eye on her. You'll hear from me tomorrow."

Ian thought for a few moments after he finished on the phone. He had a sudden inspiration and called Julia's hotel. She wasn't in her room so he made another call instead. A few minutes later he left, with instructions to his secretary that he would not be available until the next morning.

. . .

Jill went straight back to her house after returning the gear to the dive shop. She first thought she'd been careless when she found the door unlocked, but changed her mind when a tall, mustachioed man stepped into her path as she entered the main room. She turned to step back out and found a second, smaller man smiling at her, blocking her way.

"What do you want?" She asked quietly.

"Some information," the darker man replied.

"Who are you?" she asked.

"We ask the questions. Where did you and Miss Fairchild go this afternoon?"

"Nowhere."

"Come now! We saw you leave from the marina with Miss Fairchild. Now, where did you go?"

"Figure it out for yourself." Jill was acting much more brave than she really felt.

"Oh, so we have a tough young lady here," he said to the blond man. "As a matter of fact, we know you went to the cave. Why?"

"Julia just wanted to go in again. That's all."

"So, you did go into the cave!" He had been bluffing. "And did you find what you were looking for?"

"We didn't find anything. Why do you want to know?"

"Let's say we have an interest in Miss Fairchild and we want to be sure she doesn't get herself into trouble." He smiled maliciously.

"So, what do you want with me?" Jill was more than a little nervous by this time.

"I would suggest you stay away from your friend unless you really like living dangerously!" He emphasized the last word as he and the blond man exited.

Jill locked the door behind them and quickly dialed Julia's number. There was no answer in her room. She dialed Ian, but his secretary said he was out. She left messages for both Ian and Julia to call her as soon as they could. When she was finished on the phone, she sat down and cried.

Jack and Helen Grady had been shopping earlier and were very proud of their "treasures." Julia admired their purchases and promised herself to do some shopping as well. She really wanted to buy a necklace or two and a handmade dress typical of the area. She hadn't planned to spend so much time unraveling a mystery.

"Okay, Julia, what can we do for you?" Jack asked.

"Funny you should ask! I need you to entertain someone for me tonight for an hour or so."

"Who?"

"Martin Thompson."

"Mr. Thompson? And how are we supposed to do that?"

"I thought maybe you could invite him over to have a drink after dinner and keep him busy until 11:00, if at all possible." Julia smiled with a hopeful look on her face.

"What are you planning to do that's going to require us to watch Martin?" Jack was quite curious.

"I can't tell you right now, but it's really important to keep him busy for a while. Can you manage that for me? Please?"

"Well, I don't know," Helen started to answer.

Jack interrupted. "Sure, Julia. He did ask about fishing in Kansas, so I could use that as a lure." Jack laughed at his own joke.

"Oh, thank you, Jack!" Julia threw her arms around his neck. "Can you call him now?"

It took only a moment to reach Martin at the office and arrange to meet at the hotel lounge later that evening.

"He said he'd be delighted," Jack beamed.

"Wonderful!" Julia gave him a kiss and hurried out of the room after promising to meet for dinner at 7:00.

The sun was getting low in the sky when Julia finally got back to her room. She saw the red message light flashing and immediately called the desk. "Hello, this is room 226. Do you have a message for me?"

"Yes, a message and a note. Will you be able to come down and pick these up?"

"Certainly. I'll be right there." Julia almost ran to the lobby.

The message was from Jill, "Please call. Urgent." The words chilled Julia's heart, as she tore open the note that bore handwriting in a very pretty script. She knew it was familiar and wasn't surprised to see Ian's signature. He suggested meeting at another address instead of the hotel, to arouse less interest in their activities. Julia had to agree that his idea had some merit and mentally visualized the location he had in mind. She could ask Jill for specifics, but felt she knew about where it was. A few minutes later, she was on the phone dialing Jill's number. She got only a harsh dial tone on several tries. The hotel operator reported that the lines were out of order. He explained that he wasn't sure for how long. None of the lines on the island were operational, but it would be only temporary, he assured her. "Not to worry," was his final comment.

Julia felt a sense of discomfort about not getting in touch with Jill, but didn't have time to go to her house before meeting the Gradys. She decided to try again later and then go over in person if necessary.

Thirty minutes later, Julia was looking lovely in an almost sheer black voile dress with a knee-brushing skirt. She felt a bit daring because she was only wearing a silky camisole and tap pants underneath. She knew she looked good!

She dialed Jill's number again and was gratified to hear the now familiar gravelly ringing tone of the island's phones. There were at least ten rings before Jill answered. Julia noticed the hesitancy in her voice. "What's wrong, Jill?"

"Oh, Julia. Two men came to my house tonight and told me to stay away from you!"

"Who?"

"I don't know. I've never seen them before. I'm sure they don't live on the island."

"Are you okay? You sound hysterical."

"I'm okay. I was hysterical for a while, but I'm calmed down now. And then the phones were out so I couldn't call you again, and I didn't want to leave here alone." Jill was talking so fast Julia could hardly understand her.

"Would you like to come and stay at the hotel with me? I have plenty of room." Julia hoped she would, for Jill's safety.

"That's not such a great idea. They probably will know if I'm with you. They knew we went diving today."

"I wonder how they knew and who they are. And why did they bother you? That is, if it's really me that they want."

"I don't know, Julia, but they seemed pretty serious about this business."

"How about staying here with my friends, the Gradys? I'm sure they wouldn't mind!" Julia was obviously excited about her new idea.

"That might be okay, if it's okay with them. I really don't want to put them out."

"Look, I'm meeting them in a few minutes for dinner. Why don't I ask them and call you back. Will you be okay for a little while?"

"Of course!"

"Okay, tell you what. I'm going to let the phone ring three times, then I'll hang up and redial. Don't answer the phone for any other combination," Julia cautioned Jill.

"Got it! Thanks, Julia."

"No problem. I'll call you very soon."

Julia felt a little guilty that Jill had been threatened. After all, Jill had only been helping her. She hoped she could make it up to her in some way. Jack answered the phone after two rings. He agreed to let Jill stay with them for one or two nights, if needed. He, too, was concerned about Jill and Julia's adventures. Jack even offered to pick Jill up and have her join the three of them for dinner.

"You are a real sweetheart!" Julia was happy as she hung up.

She and the Gradys had agreed to meet at the West Indian Tavern in 20 minutes, so Julia quickly called Jill with the plans and then gathered her gear for her mission with Ian later.

Twenty-five minutes later, Julia was enjoying the music of the young black pianist in the popular tavern-restaurant. There were a number of people dining, perhaps more than usual on a Wednesday, but Julia's group had no trouble obtaining a nice table large enough for all. The atmosphere was very tropical with bamboo and wicker dominating the decor. There was even a parrot named Fred. Fred didn't seem to have much purpose in life but to screech obscenities occasionally at some guy named Henry. His former owner, perhaps?

The menu had interesting entrees. Everybody chose something different, with plans to trade bites. Julia was so excited about her escapade later that she found herself trembling and could hardly eat, even though she was quite hungry. She was also a little nervous about Jill's unwelcome visitors and wondered if they had been responsible for her own incident earlier.

At 8:45 P.M., as dessert was being served, Julia excused herself and headed for the exit. Jill caught up with her and insisted on knowing where Julia was going.

"I'm just going to meet a friend," Julia offered.

"Who?"

"I can't tell you."

"Why not? What are you up to?"

"Jill, I can't tell you just yet."

"Julia, I'm not letting you go until you tell me. I know you're going to do something crazy. You've been way too quiet tonight."

Julia thought for a moment before replying, "Okay, I'm going to meet Ian, and I just didn't want to say anything."

"Meet him for what? You haven't told me everything yet," Jill was giving Julia a tell-me-all look.

"Well, it's kind of personal…."

"Look, he's not your type! This has something to do with Linda and Scott, doesn't it? I promise not to tell, but I'm in this pretty deep too and I would like to know what's going on. So, tell me already."

"Okay, you win. Ian is going to go with me to Scott's house, and maybe Linda's too."

"Are you breaking in?" Jill seemed horrified.

"Not exactly. We have keys."

"Martin isn't going to like this."

"He isn't going to know."

"I'm coming, too."

"Jill, I can't let you get involved!"

"Julia, I am already *involved*! What's one more piece of espionage? Besides, life was dull until you came to St. Maarten," Jill smiled.

Julia smiled back. Jill was a fairly level-headed person and they could use her as a lookout. "Okay. We can use an extra person. Let me go tell Jack that I'll bring you home a little later."

Ian was a little surprised when Julia arrived with a shadow. Jill and Julia were beginning to remind him of the Bobbsey Twins, in a grown-up version. The trio drove in Ian's pick-up (less ostentatious than the Mercedes) to Scott's house first, parking about a block away. Julia produced the key and opened the back door when they arrived at the actual house.

They agreed on signals in case of problems and left Jill guarding the outside while Ian and Julia went inside. Ian had a small flashlight and led the way to the front of the house.

"What are we looking for, Julia?"

"I'm not sure. Maybe something of Linda's, maybe a note. Maybe, I don't have a clue!"

"That I would believe."

Julia considered slugging him, but resisted. They were in the kitchen looking at some papers on the table when Julia let out a squeal. "This could be something!"

Ian and Julia together read the crumpled note she'd found, after carefully smoothing out the wrinkles.

'Tanks checked. No problem. Money Friday.'

There was no name on the paper anywhere but the handwriting was masculine in character.

"Do you recognize the handwriting, Ian?"

"No. I wonder whose tanks were checked and who's got the money, and why?"

"Do you suppose this is about Linda?"

"It certainly seems like a possibility."

"Scott must have known something."

"Perhaps, but someone was careless to leave this around." Ian was scanning the room for other finds.

"Maybe they didn't even see it, because it was all wrinkled up," Julia offered.

"Well, it certainly doesn't answer any questions, and it raises some new ones." Ian turned off the miniature flashlight when he heard the tapping on the door.

Julia's heart stopped. Ian grabbed her hand and led her to a closet he'd noticed earlier when they'd entered the room. They had just closed the door, fortunately without making any noise, when the front door opened unceremoniously and noisily.

Ian peered through the keyhole of the old-fashioned closet door trying to get a glimpse of the other visitors. It was difficult because there were no lights on and the flashlight carried by one of the intruders didn't illuminate the faces well enough to see any detail.

"It's got to be here somewhere! You should have made sure you had it the last time you were here," said one voice. Ian noted that the shorter person seemed to be the leader.

"I told you...I did have it. But it must have fallen out of my pocket or something." Julia was startled to hear a British accent. Martin? No, too high-pitched. She wanted to ask Ian what he saw but it was too risky.

"Check all those papers over there. I'll check the other room." No accent on this guy. Julia wondered what papers they were looking for. She had the note in her hand. Was that it? A long five minutes passed before either voice broke the silence.

The man with the British accent was obviously frustrated. "I'm certain it's not here. I know I had it when I left here so we may as well trace my path and forget about this place."

The other voice responded, "You're probably right. Let's go."

The front door closed with a tug and click. Ian and Julia waited another minute before leaving the safety of the musty closet. Julia promptly sneezed twice.

"Thank you for waiting to do that," Ian chided.

"What was that all about?"

"Obviously, they're looking for something and it seems to be important."

"Ian, do you suppose it's this note?"

"I doubt it. I'd guess something more important than that."

"Did you know who they were?"

Ian shook his head. "Never saw or heard either one before, as far as I know. Let's look around a few more minutes and get out of here."

Neither of them found anything interesting in the next five minutes. Scott had little in the way of material possessions. The little rental house was sparsely furnished and decorated in typical bachelor style with a beer bottle here, a Sports Illustrated there, and a

Playboy on the nightstand. Julia was about ready to call it quits when she found a photo in the Sports Illustrated as she thumbed through it. Julia quickly slid the photo into her jacket pocket without mentioning it to Ian.

Ian rejoined her and shrugged his shoulders. "Anything else?" he asked.

"No. Are we going to go over to Linda's?"

"Let's do it."

Julia carefully locked the back door as they left. Jill was waiting in the shadow of the house. She could hardly contain her excitement as Ian and Julia joined her. "I nearly died when I saw those guys coming. Did you see who they were?"

"Ian saw them through the keyhole, but I only heard the voices. Did you recognize them, Jill?"

"I can't be sure. It was too dark to see much. But I think I've seen the taller guy around recently. Did you find anything?"

"Just a note, and it may not help at all because I can't tell who it's to or from. It may be to Scott, but it doesn't make sense."

"What does it say, Julia?"

Julia showed her the note as they walked to the car. Jill agreed that it wasn't much. The short trip to Linda's house was quiet the rest of the way.

They split up as before. Ian let himself and Julia in through the back door. The back light was off this time (turned off or burnt out?). The mail was still in a pile on the table as Julia had seen through the window earlier. She thumbed through it, noting that one letter was from Framingham, Massachusetts, most likely from her parents. How sad that she never got to read it.

The bedroom was neat and tidy. There were a few odds and ends scattered around, and lots of pictures of fish on the wall. Linda appeared to have been a decent photographer. Julia found herself smiling as she studied the photos. Some were very clever. Hearing Ian call her name snapped her back to the present.

She went into the small living room to see what Ian had discovered. He was holding a small pile of papers. Among the items was a receipt for filling one set of mini-50's dated the previous Thursday. It came from Underwater Sports. Scott had signed it as the agent.

"I don't see how this helps us. I already knew that." Julia waited for Ian's reply.

"Well, it just proves she had a full tank when she started out, so something happened after she picked up the tanks."

Julia didn't fully understand Ian's reasoning, but she hadn't told him of the carbon monoxide yet. The numbers on the receipt did seem to check out with one set of tanks as far as she could remember from the notes she'd taken earlier.

"Ian, we need something else. That's just not enough to prove anything! I know she had two sets of tanks."

Ian seemed surprised. "Are you sure?"

"Yes, Scott told me." Julia missed the look on Ian's face as she returned to the bedroom and pulled open the drawer on the night stand. Linda had been a neat housekeeper and very little was out of place. Julia found an address book, several envelopes with letters inside and some miscellaneous items. Out of curiosity, she flipped through the pages of the address book. She found several names she recognized: Ian, Martin, Scott and many more that she didn't know. She decided to take it with her for future reference.

There was a beautiful wooden chest on the dresser. Julia opened it, expecting to see the usual tangle of jewelry, and gasped when she saw the small packages of white powder. She had no doubt that it was cocaine. Linda apparently made a good living to support what was obviously an expensive habit. She slipped one package into her pocket for analysis later and closed the box again. She jumped at least six inches when Ian's voice broke the silence.

"Are you finding anything, Julia?" Ian asked from the doorway.

"Ian, did Linda use cocaine?"

"Why do you ask?"

"Look at this." She opened the box, and Ian let out a whistle when he saw the stash.

"That's worth some bucks!" He exclaimed.

"I'd say so."

"It's not such a big deal. Coke is popular with the jet set here." Ian shrugged his shoulders as he spoke.

"Is Linda part of the jet set?"

"No, but she had contacts who were."

"Obviously." Julia closed the box again. "Well, let's check out the rest of the house. You check the bathroom."

Julia went into the kitchen. Several letters were among the bills and junk mail (even in St. Maarten, one couldn't escape catalogues and junk mail!) on the table. The one that caught her eye had a return address in Boston. She recognized it as Tony's and surmised that it was probably something about business. There was no letter inside to confirm her suspicion, however.

There wasn't much else to see. Linda's diving gear was all on the back porch. There were several vests and BCs, various fittings, extra hoses, an old tank, extra weights, fins and so on. Nothing out of the ordinary.

"Well, Julia. Nothing in the bathroom. Is there anything else you want to look at?" Ian asked as he entered the kitchen.

"I think we've covered it. I thought there would be an answer here somewhere. It's kind of sad to be here anyway. Can we go?"

"Sure, Beautiful."

They gathered up Jill and drove back. Jill noticed Julia's subdued mood and decided to wait to ask questions until after they left Ian.

Ian left Jill and Julia at Julia's car and promised to meet them later in the week.

Jill was the first to talk on the drive back to the hotel.

"Okay, Julia. What did you find?"

"Would you believe cocaine?"

"I might…"

"A *lot* of cocaine?"

"How much is a lot?"

"Enough for about 100 people to get high on, all in nice packages, like this." She handed the one she'd 'borrowed' to Jill. "Remember the stuff we found in the cave on the second dive?"

"Yes."

"Well, I didn't think much of it then, but now I'm beginning to get a picture of Linda's other life. I wonder if Ian or Martin knew that she was using drugs. Ian didn't seem too surprised when I showed him the stash. He could be a good actor, of course. Are you still game to go looking for Linda's boat tomorrow, Jill?"

"Yes, I could leave early in the afternoon, but I could not arrange to take the whole day off. Should we take some diving gear, just in case?"

"Good idea," Julia responded.

They pulled into the parking lot. Ian's white Mercedes was in the parking lot at the far end. Julia was surprised he'd beaten her back, but then realized he'd probably left his car here when he took the pickup.

A few minutes later, after escorting Jill to the Gradys' room, she locked the door behind her and made mental notes of her new finds while she undressed. It appeared that Linda was involved in drugs in some way, but she wasn't sure it was related to her murder. The note at Scott's suggested some tie-in with Linda, but what? And why? Someone on the island was keeping an eye on her, and was trying to threaten her and Jill. She strongly suspected Martin, but didn't have any proof. Besides, he was working within the law. Ian? He had been involved with Linda, but Julia couldn't think of any ulterior motives for him killing her. Scott was dead. Was it because he knew too much about Linda, or did he get in the way of something else? And why was Linda killed? Was it about drugs?

And who wrote the note on her car, and the note at Scott's? She needed to find someone with a British accent and someone with a squeaky voice (low testosterone level? she asked herself) to match the voices at Scott's. She realized that Ian had never described the intruders and resolved to ask him about it the next day.

She wrote some notes to herself about Linda:

1. Talk to neighbors of Scott and Linda
2. Find Linda's boat
3. Ask Ian to describe intruders
4. Talk to Martin about autopsy

The last item was going to be the hardest but she knew she couldn't avoid it. Then she turned out the light and fell asleep.

CHAPTER TEN

Trouble with a Capital 'T'

Julia awoke with a start when the alarm went off. She'd had troubled dreams and the alarm fit right in with the thoughts she'd been experiencing. It had seemed like a short night. She was glad she could meet Jill at the hotel this morning because it was still 15 minutes more before she finally dragged herself out of bed and pulled on some clothes. Otherwise, she would have been late.

She rang the Gradys' room when she was ready. Jill answered. "What a sleepyhead!"

"Hey, I had important stuff to do last night!" Julia retorted.

"Like what?"

"Like sleep," Julia giggled.

"Are you ready to run?" Jill asked.

"Yes. Meet you in the lobby in five minutes."

"You got it!"

Fifteen minutes later, Julia and Jill had settled into a seven-and-a-half minute pace as they ran their usual route. Neither had said anything for several minutes when Jill asked Julia what her plans were for the day.

"Well, I need to talk to Scott's neighbors, and Martin wants me to stop by today sometime."

"Sounds like it could be a busy morning."

"Not too busy to find some time to get some sun, I hope!" Julia turned and smiled at Jill.

"Heaven forbid! But you're getting a pretty healthy tan already there."

"What about you, Jill? What time do you want to meet to look for Linda's boat?"

Jill thought for a moment. "I have to supervise a cruise to St. Bart's this morning, but I don't have to return with the guests so I should be back by 1:30."

Julia nodded. "That should be just about right."

"Julia, I wouldn't be surprised if the boat hasn't been taken care of already. Did you ask Martin about that?"

Julia shook her head. "No, I don't think he really likes to talk to me about stuff like that. He seems to think I'm too nosy. But I suppose it is dumb to go looking without checking first. I'll check with him when I see him this morning and leave you a message if we don't need to go."

"So, otherwise I'll meet you at, say 2:00? At Bobby's Marina?"

Julia nodded her agreement.

"Okay, Julia. Promise me you'll stay out of trouble this morning." Jill used her sternest voice.

"Jill, that I can't promise!" Julia protested.

They giggled as they finished their run and headed to their respective rooms, both anxious to get on with the day's events. Julia hadn't made plans to meet anyone for breakfast, but she felt a sudden urge for company. She realized she was missing Tony as she reached for the phone and called Greg at the number he'd given her earlier.

"Yeah, this is Greg," a sleepy voice answered.

"Hi Greg. This is your friendly wake-up service. What's for breakfast?"

"Is this Julia?" He sounded more awake.

"Good guess!"

"No, you just have a very distinctive voice. You have no accent!"

He laughed. "So, you want breakfast?"

"Only if you're offering to join me."

"How about *you* join me. I'd love to cook up an island specialty."

"You're kidding! That would be fun." And private, she thought. "Are you sure you want to do this on such short notice?"

"Of course. I was going to offer anyway, but I haven't been able to catch up with you." Greg paused, then continued. "Is there anything wrong? You know, calling me so early and all…"

"Oh no! Not at all! I just felt like company for breakfast," she replied somewhat nervously.

"Well, you've got it! Do you want to drive over or should I pick you up?"

"I'll drive over. I have some errands to run afterwards, anyway, so I'll want my car. How soon should I be there to eat this gourmet delight?"

"Give me half an hour, Sweetheart, and the world will be yours! Oh, and it's not formal. Casual attire will do." Greg teased.

Julia could sense Greg's smile and light bubbly spirit, and smiled. "I'll be there. Bye!"

Julia hadn't planned on Greg's invitation but she found herself grinning at the prospect of seeing him again. She was definitely attracted to him. And enjoyed spending time with him. She had some questions for him anyway about Linda and Ian and could kill two birds with one stone over breakfast. She dressed carefully with consideration for meeting Martin later, particularly. She decided to try to appeal to his masculine ego and maybe improve her chances of getting the information she wanted. Twenty minutes later when she went out to the parking lot, she found a second warning on her car.

'First there was one.
Then there were two.
Would you be upset
If the next one were you?'

Julia felt a chill through her whole body as she read the ominous message. Obviously, changing cars hadn't fooled whoever was threatening her. She felt she must be getting close to some answers, or at least somebody thought she was. The "Friendly Island" wasn't necessarily always friendly, it appeared. As she drove to Greg's house, she tried to recall all the people who might know her car. She couldn't think of all that many. Ian, Jill, the Gradys and probably some of the hotel staff, if they'd seen her get in and out. And obviously someone who liked to write rhyming notes. She decided to show this one to Ian the next time they met.

· · ·

Moments later, she hopped out of the blue Subaru at Greg's house. Wonderful smells wafted through the open door. Freshly brewed coffee and hot rolls were on the menu, for sure. His front door was wide open. Julia poked her head inside the room.

"Greg, what beautiful flowers! What a nice touch!"

"You like that, huh? Good, just what a bashful host likes to hear," Greg replied, as he held out his arms to greet her.

"Bashful? You? That's a joke, isn't it?" Julia returned his greeting with a kiss on the cheek. "Smells divine in here. Are you some kind of masculine Rachel Ray?

"No, I just like to cook a little. And breakfast is my favorite meal. Today, the chef's special is "Omelet a la Provencal." Greg did a little French waiter bow.

"Sounds fancy."

"Well, it's a little something I whip up from scratch. Eggs, of course, some cocktail sauce, shrimp, onion, mushrooms, garlic, and voila! A treat for the queen!" Greg smiled at Julia. "I do hope you're hungry."

"Ravenous!" Julia laughed.

"Good. By the way, you do look lovely this morning."

Julia found herself blushing, again, as she smiled. Hot pink was a good color for her. The pants and sleeveless camisole fit her nicely and showed off the deepening tan of her arms and chest. "Thanks, Greg," she replied as he led her to a chair in the sunny dining nook.

Birds were singing outside as the sun streamed through the flowers and vines in the small yard. Julia felt very much at peace as she enjoyed the view.

Greg produced a bottle of Champagne from a silver bucket on the counter and poured two tall glasses. "Julia, let's toast this lovely day and my beautiful guest."

"How about my handsome host?" she responded with a smile.

He shrugged, "Whatever. Let's eat!"

Julia took her first bite and was impressed with Greg's culinary skills. The food was very good, as was the Champagne.

"Greg, do you know if there was any animosity between Ian and Linda?"

"Over what?"

"I don't know, really. I gather that she was pretty much in love with him, at least at one time. Do you know why they broke up?"

"Well, the way I understand it is that Linda was pressuring Ian to get married. Ian wasn't ready to go that far. I don't think there were any big fights or anything. They were kinda letting things cool off for a while."

Julia considered Greg's answer for a moment, then asked, "What about Martin and Linda, then?"

"They were just friends. Nothing to do with love. Linda seemed to need a man around and Martin always had a crush on her anyway, but he knew her heart was really somewhere else."

"Martin doesn't seem to be grieving very much," Julia replied, somewhat confused.

"You just need to know him better. He's actually quite a gentle, sensitive person."

"Well, I hadn't noticed!" Julia replied as she enjoyed the savory omelet.

"Then you'd be surprised. He is a true defender of the underdog."

"I honestly haven't gotten that impression, so far, anyway. I've felt more that he resents my so-called 'prying into things'." Julia was a bit defensive on this point.

"Well, he's not used to assertive women, and Linda was a special person, so this is really a shock to him."

"Are you defending his behavior?"

"No, I just know him better than you do." Greg was a little surprised at Julia's apparent anger.

"Okay, I admit I may be a bit biased and don't have your background on his personality. Let's change subjects. What about Scott? Is there any connection to Linda there?"

Greg considered her question before he answered. "She kinda took him under her wing when he first came here. He got the job because of her, but I don't think there was any personal thing going on."

Julia thought about that for a moment. "I'm puzzled about why Scott was killed. I just can't make any logical connection between Linda and Scott that would be worth killing him for." Julia hoped that Greg wouldn't guess she was just fishing. She did have some ideas, but they were very sketchy.

Greg finally replied, "There's some talk that Scott had been over at Linda's quite a bit. There was a fair age difference. Ten years, I'd guess, and Linda did flaunt it in Ian's face a couple of times that I know of."

"So, do you think she was maybe trying to make him jealous? Anyway, that still doesn't make a motive for murder, unless Ian were guilty, and that doesn't seem likely."

"Hardly," Greg agreed.

"Perhaps there was some other reason…" Julia was thinking of the photograph she'd found.

"Well, I don't know what and it's not important right this minute. Can we just eat, Beautiful?" Greg flashed his handsome smile at Julia again.

"All right," Julia replied, as she realized she'd met a dead end for the time being. "Did I tell you that this is delicious already?"

"Thank you, Mademoiselle!"

They finished every morsel of food and a second glass of champagne. Julia was stuffed when she left a little later. She'd had to promise Greg a return engagement for dinner that night, but it was worth it. Now she had to find out what Martin could, or would, tell her.

• • •

Ian felt like he'd spent all morning on the phone and was enjoying his third cup of coffee when his secretary buzzed him on the intercom.

"Do you want to take a call?"

"Is it Julia?" Ian had left instructions not to be disturbed, but he did have a question to ask her if she happened to call him.

"No, it's a gentleman. Greg, I think. I didn't ask but it sounds like his voice."

"Fine, go ahead and put him through. But continue to hold other calls, unless it's Julia."

"Yes, sir. Here's your call."

"Hello, Greg. What's up?"

"Good morning, Ian. You were right about Julia. She won't stop snooping around about Linda." Greg sounded a little exasperated.

"You mean you can't keep her out of trouble, either? I'm disappointed, Greg." Ian teased Greg a little with this comment.

"Hey, man, I'm trying! But this dame has only one thing on her mind, and that's Linda. She just won't buy that it was an ordinary accident. She keeps asking questions, and they are all related to Linda."

"Okay, Greg. Just keep an eye on her. And I'll try to help out. Did she say what her plans were for today?"

"Kind of. She mentioned talking to Martin at his office, and she was apparently going to go out with Jill later today to go diving, I would guess."

"None of that sounds too dangerous. She's probably safe as long as she stays with Jill. I wish I knew how to scare her enough to stop her snooping!"

"Ian, I don't think that's possible. She has more guts than most men. And she certainly doesn't understand the meaning of the word 'No'".

"Or dangerous," Ian added, thinking of the risks she'd already taken. "Well, just do your best to keep her out of too much mischief, and for Pete's sake, don't let her know you're following her!"

"Aye, aye, Sir," Greg replied as he hung up.

Ian was pensive as he replaced the receiver in its cradle. He had lit his pipe while talking with Greg and now leaned back in his chair with his feet on the desk as he made mental notes of his progress so far. Thoughts of Julia kept breaking into his mind. He smiled as he formed a mental image of her in the sunlight at his house the day she'd worn the teal blue sundress. She was a very attractive woman and he found himself having more than a professional interest in her. He had to admit that he was flattered that she seemed to enjoy his company as well. She had mentioned her boyfriend enough that he found himself wishing Friday wouldn't come, knowing this 'Tony' person was arriving then.

The intercom buzzed again. "Yes, Connie."

"I have that phone call to Mr. Roberts now, Mr. McDonnell."

"Thank you, Connie." Ian hit the flashing light for the call. "Good morning. How are things in Boston?"

CHAPTER ELEVEN

Who Really Knows Scott?

Julia was anxious to get to Martin's office and had a somewhat heavy foot on the accelerator. She nearly ran into a car in front of the island's biggest supermarket because she wasn't paying attention. She slammed on the brakes and missed the gray Toyota by inches. While she was waiting for the Toyota to get out of her way, she noticed a white Mercedes coupe in the lot across the street. At first she thought it was Ian's but the license plate numbers weren't familiar. Ian's number was easy to remember because it was the same as her house number at home: 1213. This was 2161. She made a mental note to remember to ask Ian or Jill who it belonged to. After a couple more minutes of delay, she was finally was able to continue on her way in the traffic, which seemed to be heavier than usual for this time of morning.

Julia presented herself to Martin's receptionist and was ushered into his office immediately. He was on the phone and motioned for her to sit down. She noticed that the tanks she'd seen earlier were still in his office. That was good, she thought. She was thinking of her plans for the rest of the day when she realized that Martin was talking to her.

"Oh, I'm sorry, Martin. What did you ask me?"

"I was just curious about the autopsy report on Linda. What did you learn?"

"Very interesting findings. The lungs looked normal except for some congestion, which wouldn't be surprising from the exposure, and no evidence of emboli. And nothing physically wrong." Julia had decided to leave out the possibility of carbon monoxide poisoning for now, at least until she could locate the other set of tanks. Martin seemed noticeably relieved when she was done. Was he worried about what she might find? Or was she reading things into all of this?

"So, what was the official cause of death?" Martin finally asked.

"Hypoxia, due to presumed tank malfunction." Julia knew this was technically correct, so she wasn't actually lying, she rationalized to herself.

"Martin, do you mind if I have Linda's tanks checked independently for any evidence of malfunction?"

"No, go ahead. Whatever you can come up with will be helpful. Where were you going to have them checked?" He asked.

"Probably stateside in Miami. That would only take one day up and one day back."

"That's fine. I just need to know which shop they're going to. We'll pay the shipping costs."

"Thanks. I'll make some calls and get them on their way. Now, what more do you know about Scott?" Julia decided to test the waters since Martin was being helpful today.

Martin was taken aback just a little by the direct question, but, then, he was getting used to Julia's straight-forward style, though she was never abrasive. "Why do you want to know about Scott?"

"I just feel he had something to do with Linda and her death, and if there are any leads on who was responsible for Scott's death, it might help to solve Linda's." Julia hoped Martin would answer her question if she put it that way.

"But you just told me the official report was possible tank malfunction!"

"I said suspected, not definite, and that's only their opinion. I'm not ready to agree with that yet." Julia was firm on this.

"Julia, what will it take to satisfy you that this was an accident?" Martin was clearly frustrated.

"Martin, if this was an accident, then explain why threatening notes have been left on my car, and why my hotel room has been broken into, and why Jill has been threatened for helping me?"

"And suppose you tell me why you have kept that all to yourself? How many notes have you found? And when was Jill threatened?"

"I thought I'd told you about the first note. It was on my car several days ago. That's why I changed cars. And the other one was just this morning. Someone who thinks he, or she, is a poet." Julia fished the latest one out of her purse. "It's a little crude. Maybe we could call it 'island' poetry." Julia giggled a little as she handed it to Martin.

Martin, however, was serious in his response. "This isn't funny. It may be somebody's idea of a joke, but it doesn't strike me as a very funny idea. Did you say you found this on your car this morning?"

"Yes, when I left the hotel to go to meet Greg."

"What time was that?"

"About 8 A.M., I'd guess. No, more like 8:15 because I made another phone call after I talked to Greg, so it was a little bit later."

"Was the first note like this?"

"The words were different, but it also rhymed. It was words and letters pasted onto white paper like this one."

"What did it say? Exactly, if you can remember." Martin was very interested.

"Roses are red.
Violets are blue.
Scott is dead. No, *Lewiston is dead.*
Next could be you."

"Julia, that is a serious threat. You may be in real danger if you don't quit playing amateur detective! Let me handle this!" Martin was more upset than Julia had thought he would be. Or maybe he was just angry.

"I've been careful. Besides, you keep telling me it was just an accident, so what's there to get excited about?"

"First, I have not been completely straight with you. I, too, have been suspicious that Linda's death was not accidental, but I cannot be too vocal about that because if it is known that I am investigating a murder, my suspects will be much harder to nail."

"Do you have suspects, then?"

"I have my suspicions, but no hard evidence."

"Who?"

"Julia, I can't tell you. It is officially confidential information."

"Okay, I can handle that." Julia accepted that answer for now.

"Also, Julia, you perhaps have not been as secretive as you thought you were. Someone obviously is afraid that you are going to learn something incriminating, or even that you already have. I implore that you tell me what you know and let me take over." Martin was pleading.

Julia was beginning to believe that Martin was sincere in his concern. She wondered how much he knew about all she had been doing. And how he knew.

"How do you know what I've been up to?"

"I know you've been asking a lot of questions. It seems that everywhere I go, you've already been there!"

"So, what's wrong with that?" She was being a bit coy because she was still not entirely convinced that Martin was as interested as she in getting the real answers.

"Julia, how many threats does it take to show you? Somebody out there is serious about this business. And you're out of your league. This is not a movie. This is not a Nancy Drew mystery. This is real life. And you could get hurt!" Martin's voice was getting louder as he showed his frustration with dealing with Julia.

Julia decided to acquiesce, at least verbally. "Okay, Martin. I appreciate your concern. I'll back off. You're right, I'm not Nancy Drew. I'll behave myself. You don't have to worry about me." Julia paused for a moment, then said, "but can I still have the tanks checked out?"

Martin threw up his hands, "Yes, you can check out the tanks. I was going to do it anyway, and it will save me some time. But that's *all!*"

Julia nodded as if in agreement. Martin seemed to have forgotten temporarily that he wanted to know what else she knew and Julia wanted to be gone with the tanks before he remembered. She gathered the mini-50's as Martin opened the door to let her out.

"And, Julia, I want a complete report on the tanks. And, I still want an official printed autopsy report," Martin said rather sternly.

"Yes, sir. Thank you, Martin. I *will* be good."

She backed out through the door. Martin didn't look as though he entirely believed her, but he seemed relieved, nevertheless. Julia was elated that she finally had her hands on a set of tanks. Whether or not it was the set she really wanted, she wouldn't know for sure until later. She had decided to ask the other guy at the dive shop to recommend a shop in Miami where she could send the tanks to be checked. That was where she would head next.

When she got back to the car, she dug out the notebook she kept in her purse. It took only a few seconds to match the numbers on the tanks with ones she'd found recorded at the Dive Shop. Julia wondered if anyone else suspected there was another set of tanks. She had been feeling a little frustrated in her search for another set, not having seen any mini-50's at Scott's or Linda's. For now, she was content to have at least one set of tanks in hand to check out.

A few minutes later, she was talking to Steve at the dive shop, explaining what she needed. Steve asked, "Did you say these were Linda's tanks?"

"Yes. We're just trying to get confirmation on the cause of death."

"There's one very good shop that we've done quite a lot of business with that should be able to handle this without any problem. Can I call them and see?"

Julia smiled, "That would be terrific!"

Julia examined the European one-piece backpack/BC units as she waited for Steve to place the call. She had learned to be patient when trying to call the United States. There were only a few lines available to call out of St. Maarten and they were frequently tied up, especially during business hours. She was pleasantly surprised when Steve announced that he had gotten through to the dive shop in Miami and that they would be glad to take the tanks. Julia helped Steve pack the tanks, enclosing explicit instructions for contacting her regarding the results. She decided to take Steve up on his offer to deliver the tanks to the airport for the afternoon flight to Miami. At Martin's expense, of course.

Her next project was interviewing Scott's neighbors. She still had three hours before the appointed time to meet Jill, which was plenty of time. Julia drove her rented Subaru across the Dutch side of the island toward the lime green house where Scott had lived. All of the houses in this particular neighborhood were small and old. What the houses lacked in style was made up by the bright colors. Most of the colors in the rainbow, plus some that weren't, were represented in the dozen or so houses on this dead-end street.

Julia stopped in front of a bright yellow house next door to Scott's house. Julia's sharp knock on the door was answered by a middle-aged woman who looked tired to Julia.

"Hello, can I help you?" She greeted Julia.

Julia couldn't immediately place the delightful accent. French, perhaps. "Yes. I'm Julia Fairchild, a friend of your neighbor, Scott Lewiston. I was hoping I could ask you a few questions."

"About what?"

"About Scott."

"I don't know if I can help you, but I will answer your questions best I can. Please come in. By the way, my name is Collette Pelin." She smiled as she motioned Julia in.

Julia stepped into a sunny parlor-like room. It was done in blues and yellows, and was very inviting. Julia sat down in one of the comfortable white wicker chairs with a blue-striped cushion.

"I'm trying to learn what I can about Scott and his friends and visitors, especially the past few weeks." Julia explained her mission.

Collette smiled. "Well, he seemed very nice. He was always polite and quiet. There were not many visitors. His girlfriend was there quite often until about two weeks ago."

"Which girlfriend?"

"Linda. The one who died while diving last week. He didn't have any other girlfriends that I noticed, at least, not recently." She paused. "Wait. There was one other woman, come to think of it, but she was only there once that I saw."

"Did you know her?"

"Yes and no. I don't know her name, but I've seen her before. I don't remember where. Very pretty girl."

"When was she there?" Julia was hopeful this would be helpful information.

Collette thought for a moment. "Let's see. It was the night I went to Carol's; that's my daughter." She smiled at Julia. "So that was last Thursday. One week ago. Yes, one week ago. I remember because of the car."

"What car?" Julia was getting more curious.

"She was driving one of those fancy cars. A big white one. A Mercedes, I think. I noticed it because it looked so out of place in this neighborhood."

"A white Mercedes? Are you sure about that?" Julia was wondering who might have been driving Ian's car. And why would they be at Scott's house, since it didn't appear to have been Linda.

"Yes, I'm sure." Collette answered resolutely.

"Was the woman alone? And how long did she stay?"

"She was alone but she was gone by the time I returned about 45 minutes later, so she couldn't have been there very long."

"Okay, what about other company. Guys, maybe."

"He pretty much kept to himself. There was not much activity besides Scott going to work, and he seemed to stay home in the evening a lot. Sometimes he left with Linda."

"Were you here the night he was killed?" Julia held her breath as she waited for the answer.

"No. We went to dinner that night. I didn't know anything until the next day. I'm sorry I can't help you there."

"Did you notice anything unusual that night?"

"I can't say that I did. I wish I had but there was nothing that night, that I saw. But I think Miss McGill was home that night. Have you talked to her?"

"Not yet. You're the first. Which house does Miss McGill live in?"

"The bright blue house directly behind Scott." She pointed the proper direction. "She's home now, if you want to talk with her."

"Yes, I will, thank you. One more question. Have you seen that white Mercedes any other time?"

"There is at least one another white one on the island that looks like the same model, and I've seen it, but not here. Scott didn't run around with that crowd."

"Earlier you said Linda had been here a lot until two weeks ago. What did you mean by that?"

"Well, she just wasn't there, but maybe once the week before the died, and she normally was here several nights a week." Collette shrugged her shoulders.

"Did they have a fight?"

"I really don't know, but I suppose that's a logical assumption."

Julia looked at her watch and gasped as she noted how much time had elapsed while talking. She stood up as she thanked Mrs. Pelin for her time and information. She made mental notes of what she could see of Scott's house from the front porch and parlor as she left.

. . .

A few minutes later, Julia was explaining her visit to a young mother at the pale pink house on the other side of the lime green murder site. There was a marked contrast between this house and the one she had just left. There was much evidence of several young children in the household. Two little girls were gripping tightly to the woman's skirt. Stephanie Heinz, she'd said her name was. Julia stepped into the small living room, which seemed even smaller because of the clutter of toys and laundry. Her hostess cleared two chairs and motioned for Julia to sit down in one as she took the other.

"Thank you, Mrs. Heinz. I appreciate you taking the time to talk with me. What do you know about Scott Lewiston?"

"Are you from the police?" Mrs. Heinz asked warily.

"No, not exactly, although I have been working with the police." This was not the whole truth, but Julia sensed a reluctance to share information. Julia tried to put her hostess at ease.

"I was a friend of Scott's. I'm trying to find out what I can about him, especially over the last few weeks, because it may help us to figure out how and why he died."

Mrs. Heinz was shaking her head. "He was such a nice young man. Always doing nice things for my kids. He babysat now and then so I could get out in the evening for a while. Not many young men would do that with three young kids, but he had a heart of gold. My kids loved him!" She was clearly saddened by his death.

"It sounds like you're going to miss him. What about his company? Were there any women besides Linda?"

Mrs. Heinz frowned. "What man doesn't have more than one woman? Sure, there were a couple. Linda was over there a lot, and before Linda he had another girl, but only for a short time. I never learned her name."

"Did you ever see a white Mercedes next door?"

"In this neighborhood?" She laughed. "No, I haven't seen any of those fancy cars around here. None that stopped, anyway."

"What about the night he died? Did you see or hear anything?"

"No, I didn't even know anything had happened until two days after. He usually babysat for me on Wednesdays so's I could grocery shop without the kids, but he wasn't there that day. I found out from the other neighbor, that French lady, that he was dead. Such a shame. He helped me a lot, he did. Especially since my husband's been gone."

"Where is your husband?"

"I don't rightly know. He took off with some young girl from Anguilla and hasn't been home since. I guess the kids got to him." Her shoulders sagged a little more, if that were possible.

"I'm sorry." Julia was sorry she'd asked such a painful question.

"Oh, it's okay. We're going to be leaving soon to go back to Germany, as soon as the visas are cleared. His family will take care of us." She was smiling as she said this.

Julia felt genuinely saddened for this young woman who didn't seem to have a whole lot going for her. "I do hope things work out for you. Thank you very much for talking with me."

"You're welcome. I sure hope they catch whoever did it. This used to be a safe place to live. Imagine this happening right next door!" The young mother shuddered as she spoke. "If I can help you any more, please come back."

So far Julia had learned only a little more than she had already known. She checked her watch after leaving the house. There was time to talk with one more neighbor. Julia walked across the alley behind the Heinz house to the bright blue one-story cottage that Mrs. Pelin had pointed out to her.

She took a deep breath as she knocked on the door of the well-kept house. A very attractive young blond woman promptly answered the door. She seemed to have been expecting someone else because her smile turned neutral when she saw Julia.

"Hello, I'm Julia Fairchild. I'm a friend of Scott Lewiston. Can I talk to you for a few minutes?"

"Uh, sure. Why not?" The questioning look turned to a recovered smile as she motioned for Julia to enter.

Julia followed the blond into a small but airy room. It was sparsely but tastefully decorated. Julia decided it looked "Californian," whatever that was. Her own house in Kelso had been described several times as Californian by her friends, and this room had a similar atmosphere. Julia felt at home immediately.

"Your neighbor, Mrs. Pelin, told me she thought you might have been home the night Scott died. I wondered if you could tell me anything."

"Why do you want to know?"

Julia was a little surprised at the crisp edge to Miss McGill's voice. "Well, I was hoping to find out more about what went on that night. There's some question about how the accident actually happened." Julia phrased her statement carefully. She was trying to give the impression that she knew more than she did, hoping that the young woman could help fill in some missing details.

"I don't think I can help you. I....I wasn't home."

117

"Oh? Mrs. Pelin said she saw you here that evening." Julia was disappointed at that revelation.

"Well, I was here for a while, but I went out with a friend to a movie."

"So, you didn't hear anything, or see anything out of the ordinary?"

"No. I couldn't have…."

"How well did you know Scott?"

"Not well. I haven't lived here long. Since I work evenings and he worked days, I didn't even run into him much."

"Did you know anything about his social life?" Julia wasn't getting many answers so far.

"Everybody knew he was infatuated with Linda, but I think that was one-sided. She was trying to get even with Ian, I think, and decided to use Scott to do it. But he wasn't wild or anything like that, if that's what you're asking."

"Thank you. One more question. Have you seen a white Mercedes around here recently?"

She hesitated an instant before she replied with a simple "No." She then quickly escorted Julia toward the door. "I have to get ready for work, if you don't have any more questions."

"Sure, no, that's all. Thank you very much. By the way, what is your name?"

"Sheila." With that, she pulled the door closed and latched it. The interview was over. Julia had the very definite feeling that Sheila knew something she wasn't telling. She had seemed nervous the whole time Julia was there and certainly knew something about a white Mercedes, despite her negative response. Julia was going to have to learn more about Sheila McGill.

CHAPTER TWELVE

Rub a Dub Dub

Julia checked her watch. She still had an hour and a half before she was to meet Jill. She'd had such a big breakfast that she really wasn't hungry yet. She decided to use the time to get some sunshine. Her sleuthing was taking a lot of her vacation time and she only had three more days before heading back to rainy reality in Washington state. She hopped into her Subaru, turned the ignition key and headed for her favorite beach.

Fifteen minutes later, Julia was stretched out on the beach with her mystery by Agatha Christie. She'd only read 40 pages so far and was eager to get deeper into the story. She was glad she'd thought that morning to pack her bikini and shorts in her beach bag so she wouldn't have to return to the hotel before she met Jill. The sun was warm on her back and she was enjoying her book. Even being in the middle of solving her own mystery couldn't keep her from enjoying a book by her favorite author.

Thirty minutes passed quickly. Julia hooked the back of her top and turned over on her back, where she found herself staring up into Greg's face. "And how long have you been standing there?" Julia asked as she smiled and looked up at Greg.

"Long enough to appreciate the view. I thought you had all kinds of pressing things to do today," Greg smiled back.

"I did, and I do. I'm already done with some of them. And I'm not meeting Jill until about 1:30, so I'm killing some time. And why aren't you at your job?" She asked him.

"I've got everybody working on taking inventory and there's no customer activity right now, so I decided to get a little sunshine, to cure the pale and wan feeling I've got." Greg laughed and contorted his face like he might be sick. "May I join you, Miss Doctor Fairchild?"

"Certainly."

Greg lay down beside her. "You seem to be very interested in that book. Is it good?"

"Agatha Christie is *always* good. You know, it's funny you should show up. You probably know a person I met today. Sheila McGill."

"Yes, a little. How did you happen to meet her?"

"She's one of Scott's neighbors. I was just talking to her about Scott. She seemed kind of mysterious. What's she like?" Julia shot a questioning look at Greg.

"Typical cocktail waitress. Nice body, nice clothes, smokes too much, and leads a pretty fast life."

"That sound like a bit of stereotyping." Julia was only half kidding.

"I suppose it does, but it's true. At least, about her. Why does she seem she so mysterious to you?"

"I just had the feeling that she knew more than she was telling me and that she wasn't telling me the truth when she answered some of my questions." Julia almost mentioned the white Mercedes, but held her tongue.

"So, what do you think she knows?" Greg asked.

"I think she saw or heard something the night Scott died. Mrs. Pelin said she was home, but Sheila said she went out," Julia said this almost triumphantly.

"Maybe Mrs. Pelin just saw her car and assumed she was home when she was out in someone else's car."

"Maybe, but I still have a funny feeling about her. I'll check out her story some more."

Greg chuckled. "You're really into this amateur detective stuff, aren't you? You do know that Martin is working on this, don't you?"

"Yes, but I seem to be the only one that is really doing anything. If I waited for Martin, it would be a year before anything happened! Besides, he did give me permission to help him out." Julia smiled smugly at Greg as she said that.

Greg just shook his head and smiled. Julia was one sassy little chick. He couldn't help but admire her spunk. "And what's your next step, Miss Sherlock?" He was lying on his side with his head propped up with his hand, watching Julia.

"Well, Jill and I are going to check out Linda's boat this afternoon, if we can find it. In fact, I should be heading over to Bobby's Marina pretty soon," she replied, glancing at her watch. "Oh, I forgot to ask. Where does Sheila work?"

"La Samanna."

Julia was impressed. That was the most expensive hotel on the island and she'd heard that movie stars and rich people were its regular clientele. She finally said, "Pretty classy place. She probably makes good tip money."

"I suppose, and I suppose you're going to go interview her boss."

"I don't think so. I'll find out what I want to know without having to go up there."

Greg said sarcastically, "You probably will, too! Tell you what. Can I interest you in a back rub before you go? I've got a good pair of hands."

Julia giggled. "I've never refused a back rub." She turned on to her stomach and unhooked her top again. She handed her lotion to Greg and made herself comfortable. Greg was good with his hands, as he'd claimed. Julia was feeling warm all over as he moved his hands skillfully across her shoulders, down her slim back and onto her hips. He took his time when he got to her legs. Julia thought he took more time than necessary as he worked on her upper thighs, but what the heck, it felt good. After about 10 minutes, he gently helped her turn on to her back and continued the caressing movements across her shoulders, chest and abdomen. His hand lingered on her lower abdomen, which was flat and firm from her exercise program. He moved his hands down to her thighs and finally down the rest of her legs. She felt totally relaxed when he finally stretched out next to her.

Greg spoke first. "You haven't forgotten our dinner date, right?" He was smiling another big grin.

Julia smiled back, "No, of course not. Seven-thirty, right?"

"Right. I'll come pick you up."

"Wonderful…can we go dancing, too?"

"Your middle name must be Energy. You keep going and doing. In fact, I'm surprised to see you just lying here."

"Well, can't go home without a suntan." She smiled as she hooked her top up, sat up and started to put her cover-up on. "I need to meet Jill in 15 minutes, so I need to scoot."

Greg gathered his things as well and walked her to her car. He gave her a little kiss on the forehead as he helped her in. "See you later, Julia."

"Bye, Greg. Thanks for the back rub," she yelled as she started the engine and headed toward the marina on the South side of the island.

• • •

There was no place on the island that took longer than twenty minutes to get to, for the most part. Julia was at the marina in less than ten minutes, and found that Jill had already arrived. Julia hurried over to the boat and threw some gear into the cabin, then joined Jill inside the dive shop. Jill was packing the spare set of tanks that she'd left earlier to be filled.

"Hi, Julia. Are you ready?" Jill asked.

"I can't wait to get started!"

"Good. As soon as we get these tanks on board, we're ready to take off." Jill picked up one of the tanks as she spoke.

Julia stepped into the boat, ready to grab the tanks as Jill handed them over. Jill called out instructions to Julia to untie the lines from the dock, after she started the engine, then deftly guided the 17-foot cruiser into the channel, then out of the harbor to the open water.

Julia was deep in thought as the bright red boat skimmed across the shimmering blue water. The deep blue sky was cloudless. The breeze created by the boat moving across the water felt good on an otherwise very warm day. From their previous trip, she knew it would take about 30 minutes to reach the cave site. Julia wasn't sure what they'd find aboard Linda's boat, providing they could even find it. There were still quite a few missing pieces of information, with a motive for killing Linda being one of the big ones. She mulled over the bits of information she'd collected so far and tried to make it all mean something. She knew there had to be a big clue somewhere, if she only knew what she was looking for. Julia's thoughts were interrupted by a shriek from Jill.

"There's *Angel*!" Jill screamed.

"Who or what is *Angel?*"

"Linda's boat! That's what she named it. I guess because it was mostly white."

They were still a long way from St. Bart's. "What is it doing clear out here? We must be a couple of miles from land." Julia was puzzled.

"I'm not sure. Most likely, the anchor didn't hold and it just drifted out here. I'm going to try to get right alongside it and let you take control of it. Do you know how to drive one of these?"

"Yes, a little bit."

"Good. I can explain the basics in a minute. Now, when I'm parallel to *Angel*, be ready to jump when I yell, 'Now.' Got it?" Jill asked.

"I'm ready," Julia nodded.

"Okay, here we go." Jill skillfully guided her boat alongside Linda's boat. Julia's hands were sweating as she waited a little nervously to make the jump.

Jill yelled "Now" as she put the throttle in neutral. Julia scrambled across to the bigger boat and made a quick assessment. There was a key in the ignition. Julia turned it but nothing happened. She tried several times more and was encouraged when the motor sputtered and finally started, but it promptly died again.

She was priming the motor again, when Jill called, "Don't worry. You've probably just flooded it. Pull the anchor up while you're waiting. I'll just circle around you."

"Right."

Julia placed the throttle in neutral and stepped over the diving gear in the boat toward the anchor. She was taken a little by surprise when nothing moved as she started to haul in the one-inch line. It finally dawned on her that the anchor must be hooked on something underwater. She pulled as hard as she could but couldn't release it. She finally gave up and shrugged her shoulders at Jill, who had noticed her difficulties.

"It won't budge!"

"Damn!" Jill had a disgusted look on her face to match her exclamation.

"Why don't we just cut it off? Anchors are replaceable," Julia asked.

"True, but they cost money. One of us can go down and disentangle it."

With that, Jill began to maneuver her boat parallel to Linda's. She threw two tie-down lines to Julia, who used them to join the two boats loosely together, and then hopped into Jill's boat, which was now silently bobbing in the water. Jill was already pulling her gear on—back pack with BC, tanks, weight belt, fins, mask and snorkel.

"Julia, I'll be back in a few minutes. I'll pull on the line if I need anything."

Jill checked her gauges and entered the water from the side of the boat. Julia was a little disappointed because she had wanted to dive, but she told herself she was being silly, especially since this was a *must* dive, rather than a fun dive. She watched Jill for as long as she could see her in the water. Then she watched her bubbles. She finally turned her attention to checking out Linda's boat. She scrambled over the sides of both boats into Linda's bigger boat. A quick survey of the main deck failed to reveal anything unusual. She saw no sign that anything had been disturbed. There were several 70-pound steel tanks and another set of mini-50's neatly arranged in one corner of the deck next to the cabin.

Inside she found a half dozen or so sets of BCs, regulators, fins, masks, and snorkels and other support gear. Julia surmised that Linda had a brisk side business of guiding divers, judging from the amount of gear on board. She turned her attention to a duffel bag which lay open on the bench. She sorted through some clothes, towels and personal items, and then found a folded piece of paper that looked familiar once she opened it up.

It read: *"Rub a dub-dub.*

Two girls in a tub.

One fell out.

One less to scrub."

Julia was sure it had something to do with the cryptic messages that had been left on her car earlier. She could make no sense of it. In a way, it was ominous, but there was no actual threat. She wondered if Linda had been getting messages for a while, or if this had been the first one. She was hoping Martin knew the answer, and that he would tell her if he did. She searched through all the papers and junk on the small table and bench but didn't find anything else worth keeping. A glance at her watch told her that Jill had been underwater ten minutes already.

Julia stepped out onto the deck and stretched her body out in the sun while she waited for Jill. The sunshine felt wonderful on her skin, but she began worrying that Jill might be in trouble when another five minutes passed without a sign of her friend. She couldn't imagine that unsticking an anchor would take so long, without Jill coming up for help. After waiting another five anxious minutes, Julia decided to check on Jill. It was convenient that Jill had picked up her spare tanks because Linda's tanks were all low on air.

Julia made a final check on her gear and made a backward entry into the water. She followed the anchor line down to about 60 feet and found that it was hanging free. There was a submerged reef about 50 feet away that Julia supposed had been holding the anchor. The real question was where was Jill? Julia was concerned that Jill might have gotten into trouble like Linda. She instinctively headed for the island, after checking her bearings.

There was no sign of Jill for the next ten minutes. Julia was just considering heading back to the boat when she spotted Jill several hundred yards away, coming toward her. Julia felt a huge sense of relief as she swam a little faster toward her friend. She was within 50 feet when she began to have trouble getting air. She switched the tank to reserve and still had no air. She signaled to Jill as she swam toward her, and then blacked out.

CHAPTER THIRTEEN

Blind Fish Don't Talk

The first thing Julia saw when she opened her eyes was Greg's face above hers. Everything was fuzzy for a minute or so, and then she started remembering.

"I ran out of air, and the reserve didn't work. I thought I was going to die!"

Jill said, "I thought we were both going to die. I couldn't get you to let go of your regulator to give you mine!"

"What are you doing here, Greg?" Julia was very curious that he should be Johnny-on-the-spot, again.

"Well, from what Jill says, I gather we're here for the same reason. Martin asked me to find Linda's boat and bring it in if I could find it."

"Martin did? Today?" Julia sat up, feeling a lot better.

"No, several days ago, but this is the first chance I've had to really look. Why are you so interested in Linda's boat?" Greg asked Julia with a lot of emphasis on his words.

"The same reason as Martin. I thought there might be some clues."

"And?" Greg asked with a raised eyebrow.

"I guess I was wrong. Hey, I'm really sorry about scaring you all. I'm fine now. Let's get this boat back." Julia wanted to avoid any more questioning for the time being. She thought of one more question for Greg.

"How were you planning to get two boats back if you found Linda's boat?" Greg didn't have to answer because at that moment, a very pretty, very blond young woman stepped out of the cabin of Greg's boat.

"This is my cousin, Pam. She's visiting for a week or so. She came in unannounced this morning." Greg answered the unasked question as though he could read Julia's mind.

"Hi, Pam. I'm Julia, and I usually am not so accident-prone." She laughed a little nervously.

"These things happen, I understand. I'm glad you're okay."

"As am I," added Greg. "Pam and I will go on back and take Linda's boat in. That will save you a little time." He saluted to Julia and Jill.

• • •

Once Greg and Pam were on their way, Julia and Jill turned their attention to returning to the marina as well.

"Hey, Jill, can I see the tank I just had on? The gauge was reading 'full' when I started."

Julia checked over the gauges. There appeared to be plenty of air but when Julia breathed on the regulator, there was none.

"It looks like a malfunctioning valve. Jill, have you had trouble with this tank?"

"No, not up until today. I will definitely have it checked as soon as we get back. Are you sure you're okay?"

Julia was reflecting that there could certainly have been a different ending to this adventure. She decided to cancel that thought. But why was Jill coming back from the direction of the cave?

"Jill, what took you so long?" She chose not to mention the cave for now.

"This is really dumb, but when I was unhooking the anchor, I scared up a school of possible blind cave fish. They're getting rare around here as we get more and more civilized, so I wanted to see if I could find their hide-out. That's what Linda was trying to prove, that they lived in underwater caves right here. I followed them and didn't realize how long I was under. I certainly didn't mean to alarm you."

"Oh, Jill, I'm sorry. I shouldn't have gone after you, being unfamiliar with the area, but I was worried that something had gone wrong. I didn't think releasing the anchor would have taken that long."

"You're right. It didn't take more than a couple of minutes, and I shouldn't have gone without telling you, but it was just an impulsive action when I saw those fish. I'm so sorry I scared you. I won't even think about what might have happened."

"Please don't. You're not going to tell Ian about this, are you?"

"I won't, but Greg and Pam might."

"I'll talk to Greg myself when we get back. You know, I don't think I'll dive for a day or two." Julia said as she turned to Jill.

Jill nodded her head in agreement. "That's probably a wise decision."

• • •

Thirty minutes later, Julia and Jill had finished mooring the boat, and were ready to head home. Julia spotted Greg inside the dive shop, said a quick "good-bye" to Jill, and went to join Greg.

"Is our date still on?" she asked.

"Are you up to it?" Greg looked concerned.

"Yes. You promised we could go dancing! Um, you're not going to tell Ian about this afternoon, are you? Please?"

"Well, now why shouldn't I tell Ian? Or should I ask, why would I?"

"I know that you two are friends, and he seems to get over-excited about things."

Greg smiles. "Not necessarily over-excited, considering what you've been up to so far, Miss Julia."

"And there really was nothing to worry about!" Julia replied rather urgently.

"Julia, that was too close, but I won't tell Ian, unless you give me cause to."

"That sounds like a warning," Julia teased.

"No, that's a promise. You keep those sparkly eyes of yours out of trouble. I don't want to eat dinner by myself tonight!" Greg gave her a hug as he said the last.

"Yes, Sir. Is 7:30 still okay with you?"

"I couldn't wait a minute longer."

• • •

Julia had mixed emotions as she drove back to the hotel. Her headache was slowly going away. She was quite curious about the gauge on the tank. She decided to talk to Steve at the dive shop herself in the morning, when she checked on Linda's tanks that had gone to Miami. She was excited about learning something about that.

She was also excited to see Greg. She was more attracted to him than to Ian, and in fact, was feeling guilty because she found herself wishing that Tony wasn't coming in one more day. She'd felt intensely jealous momentarily when she'd first seen Pam and had been immensely relieved to know she was just a cousin. She mentally reviewed the clothes in her closet at the hotel, and smiled when she recalled the slinky black jumpsuit, just waiting to be worn.

The telephone message light was flashing when she walked into her room.

"This is room 311. What is my message, please?"

"Yes, Miss Fairchild. Shall I read it to you?"

"Yes, please."

"The message reads: 'Will be in Saturday morning about 10:00. Meet you at hotel. Tony.' "

"That's all?"

"Yes, Mademoiselle. The message was taken at 4:30 P.M."

"Okay, thank you." Julia frowned as she ended the call.

She was a little disappointed that Tony would be delayed another day, but also relieved that she had another day before she had to give up seeing Greg. *and* another day to do her detective work. A glance at her watch told her it was too late to try to call Tony at the office, and she doubted she'd catch him at home. She decided to call him in the morning instead.

Julia was dressed and ready to go when the room phone rang.

"Hello, Beautiful. How are you feeling after your close call?" It was Ian's voice, not Greg's as she had expected.

"I feel fine, Ian. How did you hear about it?"

"I saw Greg at the Oyster Pit. He looked a bit worried and I dragged it out of him. Are you sure you're all right?"

"I'm sure. I wasn't down very deep and Jill got me up to the surface right away."

"I'm glad. I hope you're not diving for a few days. You really shouldn't."

"I know. Remember, I'm the doctor. I'll be a landlubber, or at least stay on top of the water for the next few days. I really do appreciate your concern." Julia was feeling a little guilty talking to Ian when she would be seeing Greg in just a few minutes.

"Julia, will you have time to talk with me sometime tomorrow?"

"About what?"

"Several things...Linda for one. Can you meet me at, say 10:00 A.M.?"

"Sure. Where? Your office?"

"No. I'll pick you up at the hotel. We can go for a drive to the other side of the island."

"You got it. I'll be ready."

"See you tomorrow, Julia. Ciao!"

"Ciao, yourself." Julia smiled as she hung up. Ian's accent was irresistible, and she was always interested in knowing more about Linda.

She checked herself in the mirror one last time. She liked the look of the silky black jumpsuit. It had a deep v-neckline showing cleavage in the front, and was nipped in at the waist. It really showed off her tanned, athletic body. The red silk belt and earrings added just the right touch of color. She touched up the blusher on her cheeks and lipstick on her lips and headed out the door to meet Greg in the lobby.

Greg let out a long, low-pitched whistle when he saw Julia. "Hello, Gorgeous! Let's just skip dinner and go on over to my place."

Julia grinned. "I accept that as a compliment, but I'm starving. Let's go eat!"

"Well, if you insist. They are expecting two hungry people at the Rusty Pelican in about 15 minutes. Shall we go?" He offered his arm.

• • •

Dinner was delicious. Julia felt a little lightheaded, as they had nearly finished a bottle of Chardonnay. She was drinking her last glass very slowly.

"So exactly why did Martin send you out to look for the boat today?" She asked between sips. "I was still groggy when you told me earlier."

"He didn't actually send me out today. It was my idea to go out this particular day, so I could kill some time for Pam. And that way I would have a second driver to bring it in. He had already located the boat and knew it was safely anchored, so it could be brought in anytime. It was purely accidental that I was there when you were in trouble."

"And I'm glad you were."

"You kept saying something over and over, like 'roses are red'. Does that mean anything to you?"

"Greg! I almost forgot! Yes, I found a note on Linda's boat. See if this makes any sense to you.

"Rub a dub-dub.
Two girls in a tub.
One fell out.
One less to scrub."

"Lousy poetry."

"I had the same thought. I wouldn't have paid attention to it, but I think the same lousy poet wrote the notes that have been left on my car."

"What notes?" Greg's interest increased.

"Just a couple of garbled nursery rhymes, like someone's trying to scare me."

"Julia, Linda is dead. Doesn't that scare you?"

"A little, but I don't really think I know enough yet for whoever's been watching me to do anything drastic. Besides, I'm almost always with somebody."

"You have been covering yourself, haven't you?"

"I learned it all in books," she grinned. "I do think that someone killed Linda, and maybe that same person killed Scott, too. I don't know why yet, but he or somebody associated with him, and/or her, I suppose, is obviously keeping an eye on me."

"Do you have any suspects?" Greg was curious about who might be on her list.

"I thought of Martin, but he seems to be above-board. It could be anybody around the dive shop. And I know she has an ex-husband, but he doesn't seem likely, although I've considered a rage of jealousy because Scott and Linda had been seeing each other. Then there are plain kooks. I just don't think it was an accident. Scott was certainly not an accident."

"You're pretty much covering the basic categories: Lover, former lover, and kooks. There are also business associates."

"Such as who?" Julia asked, somewhat surprised.

"I guess the dive shop fits that category," Greg offered.

"Sure, and what about customers from her guide business?"

"That's a thought. It would be hard to track down most of those people. Linda's business was very low-key. I'll bet she didn't even keep any records of whom she took on the dives." Greg slammed his fist into his knee.

"You're probably right, unfortunately. I wish I had the answers."

"Julia, this is not your problem. There is no reason that you should feel bad. Let the authorities handle it. Please!"

"Greg, I know you're right. I just can't shake some feeling of responsibility because of having those papers in the first place. It's like I let Tony down because I couldn't keep my half of our agreement."

"Is that your fault?"

"No, but..."

"No 'buts!' You should feel lucky you haven't been killed. What if you'd been found dead instead of Linda? Or in addition to?"

"Let's not talk about that."

"You're right. Let's not."

"Okay. Sheila McGill. Where does she fit into all this?"

Greg seemed surprised at the name. "I didn't know she did."

Julia smiled. "Maybe she doesn't, but she was very evasive when I asked about Scott, and where she was that night."

"That doesn't mean anything. Maybe she thought you were being snoopy and asking too personal of a question. After all, you're not a cop or anyone officially involved in this."

"Okay, you have a point. I hadn't considered that angle."

"Not to change the subject, but when is this 'boyfriend' of yours coming to town? You've talked about him all week, but I'm beginning to think he's a figment of your imagination. Maybe that's just a line you use to keep men from pestering you."

Julia smiled again. "That would be a clever idea, but he does exist. Maybe I shouldn't call him a boyfriend, exactly. Last time I spoke with him he said he would be here Saturday, finally. He got tied up in Boston, I guess."

"He's making a mistake letting you loose among all these horny men on this beautiful island! Maybe someone should explain the birds and bees to him!"

"Believe me, he knows about them! Hey, what about the dancing you promised me?"

"Well, Beautiful, I just happen to know a little place that has the right atmosphere, soft lights, music, and not too crowded."

"If you're describing your apartment, I hope you have a second choice. I really do want to dance."

"Okay, then. Studio 7 is holding a place for us. Shall we go?"

"I think you were baiting me!" Julia grinned as they got up to leave.

CHAPTER FOURTEEN

Bumper Cars

Studio 7 was not terribly busy, but it was still a little early in the evening. Nothing got rolling until close to midnight at the discos and casinos. And it was also a week night. The island was much busier on the weekends, starting on Friday. Julia and Greg made their way to a corner table that had a "reserved" sign on it, and then went directly to the dance floor. The music was a lively calypso. Julia was delighted to find that Greg was a very good dancer. They twirled and swirled their way through several selections before they mutually agreed that they were too thirsty to continue.

"Julia, you're a marvelous dancer!"

"Thank you, Greg. I *love* to dance!"

"And it shows. Hey, there's Jill and Ian!" Greg pointed across the room and then guided Julia to their table.

"Hello, Miss Julia. So, *this* is why you stood me up tonight," Ian began teasing in that sexy British way.

"I didn't stand you up!" Julia protested.

"Now, now. I'm quite certain we agreed on dinner tonight. Didn't we, Jill?"

Jill nodded her head. "We did, Julia."

Julia shrugged in embarrassment as she remembered the brief exchange from the previous day. "It seems so long ago. I simply forgot. I'm so sorry."

"Hey, it's okay. I forgot myself until I talked to Jill this evening. Then I called your hotel and you were already out. So, I didn't worry about it. You're off the hook this time." Ian kissed Julia on the cheek. "However, I am a little envious that you'd prefer Greg's company to mine. I'm a much better dancer."

Greg broke in, "Yeah, better than you used to be. Don't worry, McDonnell. I'll take care of her tonight." He pulled Julia closer to him.

Julia finally spoke up, "Okay, end of Act I, Scene I. Hi, Jill. Does this mean you're going to be too tired to run with me in the morning?"

"Oh no! I'm never too tired to run. Besides, I'll need to metabolize quite a few calories after the huge meal we just had." Jill puffed out her cheeks to make her point, as they all laughed.

"Likewise!" Julia puffed out her cheeks too.

"Well, if you two ladies are going to run, I better get this little lady home at a decent hour." Greg smiled down at Julia.

"Ciao!" Jill and Ian replied almost together.

Once in the car, Greg headed the opposite direction from Julia's hotel. When she noticed and commented, he replied, "That place I told you about with soft music and no crowds is still open. Are you game?"

"And the bartender is named Greg…."

"Something like that."

"Tell you what, Greg. I'm super tired after today, otherwise I'd truly love to join you. But can I have a rain check this time?" She looked up at him with her baby blue innocent eyes.

"Well, I don't know. It's a very limited offer…but for you, okay."

"Thank you, Greg. You're a sweetheart."

• • •

The message light was flashing when she entered her room.

She called the main desk and the clerk read the message to her. "Call Ian. 5-4326."

"What time was the message taken?"

"11:14 P.M., Mademoiselle."

"Tonight?"

"Yes. I took it myself."

"Okay, thank you." What would Ian want at this hour, she asked herself as she dialed the number.

The phone only rang twice before Ian's familiar voice answered. "'Ello".

"Ian, this is Julia. What's up?"

"Hi, Gorgeous. I have some information that might help solve your mystery. Can you meet me somewhere?"

"Now?"

"Yes. I can't tell you over the phone."

"Okay, where?"

"You know where my office is, right? Meet me at the north end of the building. My pickup truck will be parked there. The door will be unlocked. Just come in."

"Okay, give me 15 minutes to find it in the dark."

"You got it."

Julia felt a little nervous and excited. She was dying to know what Ian had to tell her, but a night-time meeting seemed very sinister. She pushed her doubts aside, changed quickly into capris and a t-shirt, and fairly ran out the door. She could feel her heart palpitating as she drove the empty streets to Ian's office. It looked more like a warehouse, she thought to herself. Ian's truck was already there. She bravely got out, went up the four stairs, and tried the door. It opened. She was relieved to see Ian waiting for her in the hall.

"Am I glad to see you!" Julia exclaimed as she practically flew into his arms. "My imagination went wild while I was driving over here. What do you have to tell me?"

"Whoa! You're talking so fast I can hardly keep up!" Ian laughed.

"Yes, I talk too fast a lot. What did you want to tell me about Linda?"

"It isn't exactly about Linda, but it is about Scott. Martin just got some Interpol reports that he was wanted for murder in South Carolina."

"You're kidding!" Julia's eyes were wide with surprise. "Are you suggesting Scott killed Linda? But then who killed Scott?"

"Apparently Scott and Linda knew each other in the past. She may have known too much. Or maybe they had a disagreement." Ian shrugged his shoulders.

"But who killed Scott?" Julia asked again.

"Martin thinks someone followed him down here. Those thugs we saw may have been trying to cover their tracks. I know they weren't locals."

"Why are you telling me this, and why at this hour of the night?"

"Look, Beautiful. First, I'm worried that your amateur detective stuff is going to get you into deeper trouble. And it looks like we have the mystery solved with this new information. Second, I need to go to Miami tomorrow and will be leaving early, so I had to tell you tonight. Besides I knew you'd want to know and I wanted to be the one to tell you. In fact, if you hadn't stood me up earlier, I would have told you at dinner." Ian grinned as he rubbed that one in.

Julia softened with that last remark. "Okay, you win. I understand. And I didn't mean to stand you up. I swear!"

"I believe you. Now give me a hug and kiss and I'll forgive you."

It was a long moment before either of them broke off the kiss. Julia was very attracted to Ian, and knew it was a mutual feeling.

Ian spoke first. "Beautiful Miss Fairchild, I would love to take you home with me tonight and finish what we've started, but we must both get up early, so I will let you go home instead. But we will finish this later. When is your friend 'Tony' coming now?"

"Not until Saturday."

"Good. I will return late tomorrow afternoon and call you. Do you think you can be good until then?" Ian smiled as he asked.

Julia smiled, "I'll try. Do be careful and come back safely."

"I was just going to say the same thing to you. Be careful going home tonight. The roads are not well-lighted."

"This is true, and yes, I'll be careful."

Ian kissed her again before he walked her to her car. He waited until she had started the engine and backed up before he re-entered the building. He quickly dialed a number and said, "She just left."

. . .

Julia was about halfway back to her hotel when she noticed headlights in her rear-view mirror. They seemed to be approaching very quickly. She prepared to move to the right to allow them to pass. When the headlights were only a few hundred feet away, the other vehicle still hadn't slowed down. Julia thought that maybe the other driver simply hadn't noticed her and slowed down deliberately to try to force the other car to pass. She controlled the panic she felt as the other car continued to move at a high speed, and finally skimmed past her car, forcing Julia to pull onto the narrow shoulder.

She waited a few seconds before pulling back on the road, her heart pounding. She had mentally recorded the car's license number as it passed and planned to track it down in the morning through Martin. Julia had just made the left turn by the main supermarket when she saw another car coming behind her from the side street that she'd passed. It quickly came very close behind her, then stayed right behind her car. Julia was a bit annoyed and slowed down to encourage him to pass, but instead, she felt a bump on her rear fender. She instinctively swerved to the right and the other car went on by. She considered stopping and checking the damage, but with the last episode in mind, decided to wait until she got to the safety of the hotel parking lot. The car was insured anyway. She hit the gas and kept an eye on the other car as it pulled over to the right. Julia was angry, but too scared to stop. The other car pulled back on to the road behind her and stayed very close again. Again, she was bumped from the rear. This guy must be drunk, she thought to herself. She maintained control of the car and kept going. She was only a mile or so from the hotel. The other car had dropped back again, but suddenly started coming faster toward Julia again.

Julia was really frightened and prayed silently that she would get to the hotel without a serious accident. Just then, the other car sped past her. She noted the license plate number. It was the same car that had passed her earlier! The hotel was in view now, and Julia breathed a big sigh of relief. She parked the car and hopped out. She was shaking as she quickly surveyed the damage. There was nothing major, but there were certainly some dents and scrapes.

Once back in her room, Julia collapsed into the chair by the window. She was both angry and scared. Tears overcame her as she thought of what might have happened. The questions in her mind were 'Who?' and 'Why?' When she'd regained her composure, she picked up the phone and called Greg, even though it was well after midnight. He finally answered after four rings, with a very sleep voice.

"Greg, it's Julia. I'm sorry to wake you up, but I….I…"

"What's the matter, Julia? You sound upset."

"Oh, Greg. I'm so scared!" She told him what had happened, between sobs.

"You haven't reported this yet, have you?" he asked.

"No, I thought I'd talk to Martin in the morning. I got the license plate number."

"Good for you. Yes, it'll keep until morning. Are you sure you're okay? Do you want me to come over?"

"Thanks, but no, I'm fine. It helps to talk to you about it." Julia was sobbing just a little.

"You realize this wouldn't have happened if you'd stayed with me. Hey, what were you doing out there anyway? I already took you home once!" Greg was wide awake now.

"Ian wanted to tell me something, so I met him at his office. I guess it was dumb, but it was about Linda and I didn't want to wait until tomorrow night to hear what it was. He said he didn't want to tell me on the phone."

"Was it worth almost getting killed?"

"That's not a fair question. How could I know that some crazy driver would be on the same road? This was probably just an accident. The guy seemed to be drunk." Now Julia was being defensive again.

"Okay, I'm not trying to give you a hard time. I just don't like the thought of your pretty little body being all broken up on the street, and you have certainly had more than your share of close calls this week."

"Agreed. I'm sorry for reacting that way. I do appreciate your concern."

"You're sure you don't need company tonight?"

"Believe me, I'd love your company, but I'm okay now, and I have an early date to run with Jill."

"Okay, Julia. Remember, you still have a rain check. Sweet dreams."

"Thank you and good night, Greg." Julia replaced the receiver.

Julia felt a lot better after talking with Greg. She undressed, crawled into bed, and fell asleep almost instantly.

CHAPTER FIFTEEN

Three Blind Mice

The next morning as she and Jill finished their three miles, Jill asked what Julia's plans for the day were.

"Well, I have to talk to Martin again, and I promised Jack and Helen Grady that I would join them for lunch."

"Why do you need to talk to Martin?"

"He's been bugging me about the final report on the tanks we sent to Miami. And I need to report a crazy driver."

"What crazy driver?"

Julia related the story briefly.

Jill responded, "I thought you seemed more tired than usual. What did Ian want?"

"He had some information to share and he was taking off early today, so I met him last night."

"What did he say?"

Julia's intuition told her to say as little as possible to satisfy Jill's inquiry. "Actually, he didn't tell me anything I didn't already know. It was a wasted trip. What about you? Do you have a dive set up today?"

"Yes, this morning. As a matter of fact, it's a big job, so I'll make a little money, too." Jill was smiling as she said this.

"That's great! Well, time to go back to the hotel. I'll try to catch you later. Maybe we can do something tonight to celebrate Friday!"

"Sounds good. See ya!"

Julia waved good-bye as she popped into the lobby with a big grin on her face. She had some ideas of her own about Linda and Scott and could hardly wait to test them.

An hour later, at 7:30 A.M., Julia decided it was a reasonable hour to call Jack and Helen. "Good morning, Mr. Grady. This is the last call for breakfast."

Jack laughed. "Julia, I'd know that voice anywhere. What's on your mind?"

"Lunch."

"Lunch? You just said this was the last call for breakfast."

"Well, it is time for breakfast, but I'd like to meet you two for lunch. Are you free?"

"I think so, just a minute while I check with Helen." He was silent for a moment, then said "Okay, Julia, where and when?"

"How about the East Indian Tavern downtown? Is 12:45 too late?"

"No, that's perfect. Helen will be all shopped out by then, I'm sure."

"Great I'll meet you at 12:45 at East Indian."

Julia practically wolfed down her breakfast of cantaloupe, Gouda cheese and rye crackers and juice. She was anxious to get to Martin's office and report the car that had given her such a scare. She still wasn't sure that Martin was as aggressive as she'd like, but there wasn't anybody else to report to, and she did want to know who was driving that car. Martin could get that information from the car agency, whereas Julia couldn't.

The little blue Subaru was a bit dusty but that didn't hide the dents and scrapes from the previous night. Julia sighed as she remembered she'd have to report that, too. She almost didn't see the small piece of paper on the car seat and would have just tossed it into the garbage, but having gotten the earlier threats, she opened the folded note.

"Three blind mice,
See how they run.
Two blind mice,

144

Not as much fun.
One blind mouse,
Under the gun."

Julia shuddered. She wished she knew who was leaving the notes. Then she'd probably also know who the murderer (or murderers) was. The note was a bit damp, as though it had gotten wet somehow, but it was inside the car. It had been pushed in through the one-inch crack she'd left open the night before. She re-read the note, put it in her purse, started the car and headed to Martin's office.

The French secretary recognized Julia and smiled as she entered. "Did you wish to see Mr. Thompson?" she asked in her delightful accent.

"Yes, if he's in."

"But, of course. Go right in, Mademoiselle."

"Thank you," Julia nodded as she moved toward the door.

Martin didn't appear surprised to see her. "What took you so long?" he asked, without smiling.

"What do you mean?"

"I mean the little accident you had this morning in the wee hours. Greg told me about it already." He answered her unasked question. "Do you want to tell me what happened?"

Julia told him the details as accurately as she could recall. "Can you find out who was driving the car from the license plate number? It looked like a rental. The number was 74684."

"Yes and no."

"That's not a straight answer."

"Yes, I can find out who rented the car, but not necessarily who was driving it."

"I still don't understand."

"The person renting the car wasn't necessarily the person driving it last night. I need some time to track that down. I understand

145

there's some damage to your car as well. You'll need to report that to the agency. They'll take care of the estimates and repair. Tell them you've already talked to me about it and that I'm checking on the other car. They'll want to go after the other guy's insurance."

"It might be the same agency," Julia volunteered.

"Could be...wouldn't that be ironic," Martin grinned, sort of. "What else, Julia? You're grinning like a Cheshire cat. Do you have the second report on the tanks yet?"

"No, I'm going to call the dive shop in another hour or so. They're not open in Miami yet."

"You will report to me, won't you, Miss, er, Dr. Fairchild?"

"Yes, Sir," she saluted Martin and smiled.

"Okay, Julia. Do you think you can stay out of trouble?"

"All I can say is, I'll try. I'll talk to you later when I have that report. And after you get the information on that car."

"Fine. Good-bye, Julia." It was very final-sounding.

Julia exited quickly. She had almost told Martin about the latest note, but decided against it partly because he'd seemed disinterested in the others. And she still didn't fully trust him. She hopped into the car and headed to the dive shop.

Steve was on duty at the main counter. Julia approved of his tanned, blond good looks. He was very muscular, but slim, about six feet tall and 170 pounds. She wondered if he lifted weights.

He turned to help her and grinned broadly when he recognized her. "Well, hello, Julia. To what do we owe the pleasure of your presence? I know, you want to go on a treasure hunt dive, complete with pirates and alligators!"

She laughed. "Sounds intriguing, but I really have a much more tame request today."

"And that is...."

"Have you checked out Jill's tank yet?"

"What tank?"

"The one I was using yesterday. It seemed to have a faulty air pressure gauge. Jill said she'd have you guys check it."

"Let me check the book, but I'm sure she hasn't left anything for repairs with us in the past day or two. She generally just leaves empty tanks, almost every day."

"Please check. I'll wait."

Julia checked the display of underwater camera gear as she waited. One of the items on her "want list" was an underwater camera, or a waterproof case for her Minolta. Steve returned a few minutes later and said simply, "No tank."

"Hmm. I wonder why...well, I'll check with her later. Thanks, Steve." She didn't notice the smile leave his face as he picked up the phone.

Julia was still puzzling over Jill's tank a few minutes later when she stopped at Greg's office. She was ushered into a very comfortable office with traditional furnishing by an older but attractive woman. In her 50's, Julia guessed.

"Hi, Greg."

"Julia, what a surprise! I didn't expect to see you down here. Are you okay?" Greg came from behind his desk to greet her.

"I'm fine. I was just driving by on my way back toward the hotel and wanted to thank you for being so nice last night."

"Hey, Gorgeous. I care about you." He put his arms around Julia. "I would have done a lot more, if you'd accepted my offer of company."

She giggled. Greg was very appealing. The light blue and white striped shirt and dark blue tie were complimentary to his tanned skin and blue eyes.

"Thank you. You remind me of a knight in shining armor, but without the white charger."

"Give me an hour and I'll find one!"

"I'm sure you would. Let me tell you why I'm here."

"Shoot," Greg replied, as he motioned for her to sit down in one of the chairs.

She briefly outlined her agenda for the rest of the day, with an invitation for him to join her for dinner.

"So why are you telling me all this?" Greg asked, curious.

"Someone is watching me. I don't know who. You *have* been 'Johnny-on-the-spot' a couple of times when I was in trouble. If I have trouble today, I want at least one person, and preferably only one, to know what my plans are."

"Are you saying that you want me to keep an eye on you?"

"No, just to know where I've planned to go in case I don't show up for dinner."

"You *are* worried. Has something else happened that you're not telling?"

"I found another of those crazy rhymes this morning." She showed it to Greg.

"Ah ha! This isn't just a social call. And you didn't tell Martin, did you?"

"No, he'd just tell me to stay out of it."

"That's not bad advice!"

"Greg, I can't stop! I think I can figure it out with just a little more time!"

"Julia, it's not your responsibility. This rhyme, or whatever you want to call it, is probably not a schoolboy joke."

"That's why I want you to know what I'm doing."

"How about if I go with you?"

"That's not necessary. I'm not doing anything particularly dangerous today."

"Julia, I'm not sure you know the difference, and I wish you'd let me go with you," Greg placed his hands on Julia's shoulders.

"Greg, I appreciate your offer; I really do, and I will want your help, but not until later."

"Help with what?"

"I'm not sure yet, but I'll know after I make some visits today. Can I count on you?"

"Of course. I take it you'll call me later?"

Julia nodded. "Some time this afternoon. After 2:00. Will you be here?"

"Should be. If not, I'll leave a message where I can be reached."

"Thank you, Greg." She threw her arms around his neck and kissed him, then bounced out of the room.

Greg stood for a moment with his hands in his pockets as he tried to figure Julia out. "Impossible," he spoke out loud to himself.

His intercom buzzer rang. "Mr. McDonnell on the phone for you," his secretary announced.

"Thank you. Put him through."

"Good morning, Ian. What's up?"

"Greg, have you talked to Julia yet today?"

"As a matter of fact, she just left. Why?"

"Martin just called and asked if I had heard about Jill being threatened."

"Jill? When?"

"Wednesday night, I guess. Julia hadn't told me, but word got to Martin somehow and he is quite concerned about Julia and her damned detective work."

"What does Jill have to do with this?" Greg asked.

"Jill was threatened because of having been with Julia earlier in the day. Someone is watching them."

"Julia is concerned herself. She gave me an itinerary of her plans for today and told me she wanted someone to know in case she didn't show up for dinner."

"What did she say she was going to do? Ian asked.

Greg repeated the agenda, then added, "But I also think there was something she wasn't telling me. Do you want me to do anything?"

149

"Not right now. I need to contact the men at the warehouse to hurry up and get that shipment ready today. Roberts wants it at the pick-up point at 10:00 P.M. tonight."

"Will you talk to Constant or should I?"

"Greg, he's been informed. Your job is to keep Julia away from the hotel this evening, but there's nothing she can do today to interfere."

"Julia already invited me to dinner tonight, so that's an easy assignment," Greg snickered a little.

"Good. Keep her occupied with that gentleman charm of yours. She seems to have taken a liking to you anyway."

"I must admit, it's mutual."

"Just don't get too carried away. I can't have you mooning around on me until this project is done!"

"Well, Ian, this is one time I've actually enjoyed an assignment. Pretending hasn't been hard at all."

"Just keep your head and keep her busy. She's leaving tomorrow, I think, and things will be back to normal. Thank God! I'll contact you later, usual time."

"Right." Greg smiled as they ended the call. He was not looking forward to having Julia leave the next day, but he reminded himself that she already had a boyfriend anyway, and that she would never understand if he explained his true role this past week. At least he would make sure she enjoyed their last evening.

CHAPTER SIXTEEN

Tanks, but No Tanks

Julia went to her hotel from Greg's office and placed a call to the dive shop in Miami. She explained why she was calling to the young girl who answered. "Oh yes, John can help you," she responded, calling John to the phone.

"Miss Fairchild, that set of tanks checks out okay."

"Are you sure?"

"Absolutely."

"That can't be! There has to be a malfunction on that set. There isn't any other explanation."

"Ma'am, there isn't anything wrong with this set. I'm sorry if that doesn't help you. I'll go ahead and ship these back to you today."

"Okay. Thanks. You do have instructions for the bill, don't you?"

"Yes. I wish I could have helped with your problem, but I came up with zero." He sounded apologetic.

"That's okay. There's another angle. I just don't know what it is yet. Thanks anyway."

Julia hung up the phone and considered other explanations for the normal findings on Linda's tanks. She found the list of tank numbers in her purse and tried to piece together what she had learned. Linda had at least two sets of tanks, both of which had checked out okay. Where else could she have gotten carbon monoxide? Julia suddenly remembered the piece of metal she'd found in the cave and retrieved it from her diving wallet. She compared the numbers on it to the tank numbers she had recorded from the Dive Shop. Thirty seconds later she was out the door and on her way to talk to Steve again.

The dive shop was almost empty when Julia walked in. Steve was helping an older couple select some underwater photography gear. When he turned to see if she needed help, she motioned to the notebook on the counter. He nodded. Much to her surprise, there appeared to be several pages missing, including the one that she had just looked at the day before.

Steve's voice interrupted her thoughts. "Can I help you, Julia?"

"Steve, there are some pages missing." She pointed to the journal.

"Are you sure?"

"Yes. There are no entries from last Wednesday through Saturday, and it looks like those pages have been torn out." Julia showed him the torn margins.

"You're right! Gosh, I don't know anything about that. There's no reason for that, unless someone spilled coffee or something like that. What did you need?"

"I was just checking to see who else might have gotten air the same day that Linda got her last fill-up to see if they had any problems with their air." Julia hoped Steve would buy that one.

"Boy, I can't help you on that one," Steve was shaking his head.

"Okay. Well, thanks anyway, Steve," Julia said as she moved toward the exit.

Julia breathed a deep sigh as she scurried to her car. She had managed to write down a few numbers before Steve's intrusion. She knew without even checking her list that she had identified the tank she was looking for. Now she had to find it and have it checked. That would be the hard part, especially if it had been refilled since the accident. Julia glanced at her watch and noted that she had less than five minutes to meet the Gradys for lunch. She hurried to meet them.

Jack and Helen were seated at a table on the upper level of the building. They spotted Julia and waved.

"Hello! I'm starving!" Julia commented as she neared the table.

"We ordered appetizers, so help yourself," Jack offered.

Julia sat down and surveyed the room. There was so much intricacy to all the decor that the room seemed cozier than it really was. Everything appeared red and gold in the daylight. Two overhead fans provided a comfortable breeze in the otherwise muggy atmosphere.

"This certainly seems royal," Julia said as she dipped into the tray of Indian delights in front of her.

"And delicious," Helen added.

"Okay, Julia. What's up?" Jack finally ventured.

"Well, I need to have some behind-the-scenes help today to prepare for a meeting with Martin."

"What kind of help?"

"I think I know who murdered Linda, and maybe Scott, too, but I don't have quite enough proof."

"So, what are we supposed to do? Find more proof?"

"No. I'm going to tell Martin that I have incriminating physical evidence that will identify Linda's murderer and arrange to meet him at 5:30 P.M. I want you two to make sure that everyone at the hotel knows that I'm meeting Martin at 5:30. I'll tell Ian and Greg, too, so they can help."

Jack was puzzled. "Why?"

"I want the murderer to think that my room will be empty. I think he or she will try to break in while I'm gone."

"Why wouldn't they think you'd take the evidence with you?"

"They might, but I'm betting that since I haven't trusted Martin completely, they will figure I've left something in my room. Or they may try to stop my meeting with Martin, in which case, I have entrusted Greg to help me out." Julia seemed to be quite certain of her plans.

"Are you going to tell us who you suspect?" Helen asked.

"I can't. Just trust me for now."

"Famous last words, Julia," Jack laughed. "It's not a matter of trusting you. It is a matter of worrying that someone is going to carry through on those threats and harm you. Julia, this is a matter for the authorities. Let Martin handle it. Please!"

"Look, Jack, I only have about 18 hours on this island. Tony will rescue me tomorrow and Martin can finish up, but it's important that I carry out my plans tonight. Oh, also, I know who stole the papers from my room."

"Who?"

"Well, I don't actually know yet, but you have to make sure people think I do know."

"Julia, I think you're making a mistake."

"Jack, I appreciate your concern. You've been protective like a father should be this week, but I will take precautions. And you have to do your part."

"Julia, I know you don't trust Martin, and I have a feeling you're trying to set him up. Is that whom you suspect?"

"No comment."

"That's what I thought. Okay, we'll spread the word. Will you join us later for a drink?"

"Sure, I'd like that. Greg and I are going to dinner, but I'll tell him I have to be back early."

"Hey, we don't want to spoil your date!"

"It's not a real date. Besides, he'll understand. When Tony gets here tomorrow, you'll meet the real love of my life!"

"It's a deal. Shall we plan on about 10:00 P.M.?"

"Sounds good. I'll just meet you at the hotel in the lobby."

The waiter came with the check as though on cue. Jack picked it up before Julia could grab it. "My treat."

"If you insist, but I get to buy drinks tonight, Jack."

Jack winked.

Julia smiled and headed to the car. She had really enjoyed getting to know the Gradys on this trip. Julia thought for a moment before she started the engine.

She still needed to call Martin and Ian. She decided to swing by Martin's office and give him the report on the tanks in person, as well as make plans to cover herself for the 5:30 rendezvous.

Martin's secretary recognized Julia again and waved her on in to his office.

Martin looked up from his writing. "And why aren't I surprised to see you here?" he asked.

"I'm just making an official appearance to report that the tanks I sent to Miami checked out A-OK. Now you can say, 'I told you so.'" Julia looked genuinely apologetic.

"Ah-ha, as I expected. Now, I suppose you have proven to your satisfaction that this is beyond your expertise and will kindly leave the rest of the detective work to me and my staff." Martin was walking slowly around the room as he talked.

"Yes, Sir, except for one thing."

"And what is that, Dr. Fairchild?" He stressed her title.

"I asked my friends to circulate the news that I had incriminating evidence in my possession, and that I knew who stole the papers from my room."

"And do you?" Martin looked at her, as he stopped his pacing.

"Not exactly yet, but…"

"So, you're bluffing."

"Yes, but…"

"Amateur stuff. No one will believe that."

"I also said I was meeting you at 5:30 to discuss the case, so…."

"So someone could seize the chance to search your room." Martin finished her sentence.

"Yes! You don't seem surprised."

"Now I'll have to keep somebody posted to keep watch at the hotel, even though no one is going to be dumb enough to bite on that one." Martin sounded exasperated.

"So why bother, if you're that sure."

"I feel it's my duty to do what I can to protect you, even though I believe that your juvenile techniques are in vain. Don't worry. I'll assign someone on 'Julia Fairchild detail.'" Now he was being sarcastic.

Julia was angry that Martin was openly mocking her. He definitely did not bring out her best side. "All right, Mr. Thompson. As you wish."

"By the way, where are you going to be at 5:30?"

"Why?" Julia was a bit confused.

"If you're supposedly meeting me to discuss this, we should at least be in the same place."

"Does this mean you believe me?"

"It means I realize someone is watching you, and may be dangerous, and in fact, probably is more dangerous than you know, and if meeting you at 5:30 will keep you out of trouble for a little while, I'll be glad to play my part. Now, where would you like to meet?"

"How about Maho Reef, in the lounge?"

"Perfect. All of my constituents will be able to talk about how I meet beautiful women in bars." Martin was now being a bit sardonic.

"Do you have a better idea?"

"No. Actually, that's not a bad idea because they have a good crowd at happy hour and we won't be too conspicuous."

"Good. Maho Reef it is, then, at 5:30," Julia nodded in agreement.

"Now, ciao, Julia, and don't bother to stay out of trouble. My staff needs something to do anyway." He was smiling mockingly.

Julia gritted her teeth as she left his office. She and Martin had never hit it off. And the situation was not likely to improve anytime soon. She still had to talk to Ian about her plans so she aimed her car toward his office-warehouse. As she drove, she reflected on her conversation with Martin. It still seemed strange to her that he would act so nonchalant about Linda's death, both because he was the ranking authority on the island, and, if the rumors were true, he had been in love with her.

Julia pulled in beside Ian's Mercedes and bounced up the stairs. The receptionist in the main area took her name and asked her to wait. After a minute or so, during which time she admired the very modern, yet cozy atmosphere in the lounge, Julia was summoned. She was escorted down a long, straight hall with numerous doors on each side. They stopped at a room with a sign on it that read "Inventory Control."

Ian was talking to a young dark-haired man as she stepped in. He appeared to be a local, as they were talking in French. Julia understood enough to gather that something was rather urgent. Ian dismissed the young man and turned to Julia.

"Bon jour, Ma Cherie!" He smiled as Julia felt her heart melt. "What are you doing here?"

"Just making some plans for a little rendezvous later, and I thought you might be interested."

"Am I invited?"

"Certainly. I'm meeting Martin at Maho Reef at 5:30 in the lounge. I have some information to share."

"Why go to such trouble? Can't you just call him?"

"No, it has to be this way."

"Will you give me a clue as to why you're being so mysterious?" Ian teased.

"Actually, I've arranged to meet Martin because I think whoever is watching me will be tempted to search my room. Martin is going to have it watched."

"You really think they'll fall for that?" Ian asked, incredulous.

157

"I hope so. I'd like to get this settled before I leave tomorrow."

"What are your plans for this afternoon?"

"I need to talk to a couple of Scott's neighbors again, and I still have to find one more set of tanks."

"Linda's?"

Julia nodded. "The ones that killed her."

"But Martin already has those."

"I'll tell you more this evening at Maho Reef, Ian," she said as she headed out the door.

"Julia, stay out of trouble," Ian pleaded. He shook his head as he watched her walk down the hall. He wondered what else she'd found out and hadn't shared with him.

• • •

Julia jumped into her car and checked the time. She had to make a quick trip to St. Bart's to double check on Linda's activities that final day. She would just have enough time if she left within the next 30 minutes.

Back in her room, Julia dialed Jill's work number. "Hi, Jill, Julia here."

"Yes. Hi, Julia. What's up?"

"Jill, I need to borrow a boat for a quick trip to St. Bart's. I'll be back by 5:30. Can I use yours?"

"Sure, it's gassed up and ready to go. You know where it is."

"Great! Where's the key?"

"There's a spare one inside the shop. Steve will give it to you."

"Jill, you're a sweetheart. Thanks a million."

"Anytime."

Julia quickly got her notebook and grabbed the picture she'd found at Scott's. She was still missing an important piece of information and hoped to get closer to identifying Linda's murderer by talking with people on St. Bart's. Someone on St. Bart's Island

158

had been the last to see her alive, other than her murderer. Next, she called Greg's number.

His secretary answered. "I'm sorry, he's not in his office at the moment. May I take a message?"

"No. Yes, just tell him that Julia called. I'll call back a little later. Thank you."

Julia made a mental note to call Greg from the dive shop to arrange dinner later. She quickly changed into shorts and t-shirt, then headed out the door. The paper on the windshield didn't surprise her this time. She was more surprised when she didn't have messages at this point. She unfolded the half-printed, half-pasted-on-letters message.

"Winken, Blinken and Nod
Sailed across the sky.
Winken and Blinken met their fates.
Nod's still left to die."

She couldn't control the shudder that swept down her body. She glanced around the hotel parking lot, but didn't see anything particularly unusual. With the thought of her task at hand, she climbed into her car and took off. It was near the main supermarket of Phillipsburg, about halfway to the marina, that she noticed the white Mercedes behind her. She pulled over and slowed down, expecting Ian to do the same. Much to her surprise, the Mercedes kept going. Julia saw that it was a woman driving and that the license plate wasn't Ian's.

"I'll bet that's the white Mercedes that Mrs. Pelin saw at Scott's house," she thought to herself. She was able to follow the other car for about a mile before getting separated by the traffic as they neared the downtown area. Julia toyed with the idea of looking for the Mercedes downtown, but decided against it with her time crunch.

Just as she passed the last cross street into the downtown area, she spotted the Mercedes again. She got a better look at the driver. Sheila McGill was just getting out. The clientele at La Samanna tipped very well, if Sheila's car was any indication.

Julia drove the last few blocks to Bobby's Marina and parked her car in the large graveled lot.

CHAPTER SEVENTEEN

Who's Got the Cotter Pin

The dive shop was nearly empty when Julia entered. Steve acknowledged her right away.

"Hi, Julia. Jill said you were coming over. Do you need anything besides the key?"

"No, not right now. Thanks." She took the key from Steve and exited without any further ado.

Steve reached for the phone as she left. "She's leaving now."

•••

Julia turned the key to start Jill's boat. She felt a thrill of excitement as she guided the sleek runabout from its slip into the channel, and finally into the bay and across the blue Caribbean water to St. Barthelemy. Even though she couldn't shake the latest riddle from her mind, she found the fresh air and beautiful scenery exhilarating. St. Maarten was truly a paradise of wonderful sun and water, murders aside. As she motored across the water, she considered potential murderers. Whoever was leaving the notes had probably had a number of opportunities to stop her, but hadn't done anything specific yet. She wondered what they were waiting for, and even if they (he? she?) would carry out the implied threat. At any rate, her task at hand was to find someone who may have seen Linda the day she died, or possibly the day before. And she had barely two hours to search.

Once she landed at St. Bart's and took care of the boat, Julia started her search at the moorage office. A tall black man stood behind the counter in the office.

"Hi. My name is Julia Fairchild. I'm trying to find someone who might have talked to Linda Townsend last week."

"You mean the girl who was found in the cave?" he asked.

"Yes. Did you see her last Thursday or Friday?" Julia hoped that this man might help her.

"Let me think a minute." He put his big hands to his head and lowered his eyes. A long minute passed. "Yes, I believe so. Yes, I'm sure of it because she needed a cotter pin for something. And I didn't have the exact size she needed."

"What day was she here?" Julia asked eagerly.

"It had to be Thursday because I didn't work Friday on account of it being my birthday."

"Did she say anything or do anything else while she was here?"

"No, not as I recall. Now, wait a minute. She told me she needed air for her tanks and just as I was going to fill them, she said she didn't need air after all because there was a spare set that her friend hadn't used. So, she just took a cotter pin and no air." He smiled proudly.

"What did she need a cotter pin for?"

"Well the safety on the tank was loose because of a missing pin, so we put one on. It was not exactly the right size, but good enough for the purpose."

"Was she with anyone?"

"No, but I saw her talking to a gentleman near the boat when I looked outside." He gestured toward the pier.

"Who?"

"Can't say that I know who it was. All them white dudes look the same to me." He winked at Julia.

Julia smiled. "Yeah, I know. I'm having the same problem. Anything else?"

"That's all I remember. Sorry."

"Oh, one last question. What time was she here?"

"Um, about 3 o'clock."

"Thank you. Thank you so much! You've been a big help. If you do have anything else to tell me, will you call me or leave a message at my hotel?"

She handed him her business card with the hotel's phone number written on the back.

"Sure will," he said as he took the card and read her name. "It's been a pleasure, Miss Doctor Fairchild. Good day, now."

The "white dude" was probably Ian, knowing that Linda had worked for him that day. Julia scanned the shops on both sides of the street near the marina. There were several gift shops, two small restaurants, a marine supply store and a clothes store.

Julia headed across the street to the store on the corner. The sign over the door said *Germain's Nautique.* Once inside, Julia felt like she'd stepped back 50 years in time. Everything was dusty, and the small room was crowded with shelf after shelf of disorganized rope, pulleys, hooks and miscellaneous nautical odds and ends. She was the only customer in the shop. The proprietor was nowhere to be seen. She perused the outdated magazines in the rack for a moment, waiting for someone to appear.

No one showed up. Julia shrugged her shoulders and stepped back out into the Caribbean sun. The restaurant next door looked quiet as well, probably because it was too late for lunch and too early for dinner. Julia hoped that Linda had stopped to eat and that someone at one of the restaurants would remember her. She took a deep breath and stepped inside. A thin young girl wearing a tropical print shirt tucked into bright turquoise skin-tight jeans was taking an order from a middle-aged couple at a side table. She had tousled blond hair and wore enough make-up for three women. She looked up as Julia approached.

"Can I help you?" She had a thick French accent.

"Yes, I'm trying to find someone who might have seen or talked to Linda Townsend last week when she was here." She showed the waitress the picture she'd found at Scott's house.

The waitress studied it for a moment. "No, I've never seen her before."

"Were you working last Thursday or Friday?"

"Oui. Both days."

"And you're sure you've not seen her?"

"Oui, I am sure."

"What about the restaurant across the street? I noticed a 'Ferme' sign in the window. Do you know where I could find the owners?"

"Non, they have not opened for the season yet. She could not have been there." She was shaking her head vigorously.

"Maybe another waitress who works here?" Julia asked.

"I am the only one until high tourist season starts, another three weeks from now."

Julia pondered a moment before her next question. "Do you know where I might find the owner of the marina supply shop next door?"

The waitress finally smiled. "Mais, oui! Germain has just left here. He has cafe au lait every afternoon with Chef Jacque, then he goes back to his shop." She waved her hand towards the door.

"Thank you. Merci bien, Mademoiselle!"

Julia practically ran out of the restaurant. She had already used half of her time and still had no substantial new leads. She went into the marina supply store.

Sure enough, a small white-haired gentleman with wire-rimmed glasses stood behind the cluttered counter. Julia noted that he was wearing a clean canvas carpenter's apron over his neat khaki pants and short-sleeved shirt. Julia smiled as she considered the incongruity of his neatness amidst the clutter in the shop.

"Bon jour, Mademoiselle," he greeted her as she approached the counter.

"Bon jour, Monsieur. Parlez vous Anglais, I hope?" Julia's high school French was rusty at best.

"But of course. How can I help you?" He bowed as he answered.

"Thank goodness. My French was never very good. I'm looking for a friend, well, sort of a friend. Her name is Linda Townsend, the girl who died last week in the cave? Did you know her? Or see her last week?"

"Yes, and yes. She spent many afternoons passing time with me here. An old man, and a beautiful young lady. It's such a shame that she died. I will miss her." He shook his head sadly.

"I'm sorry. When did you see her last?"

"She came to visit on Tuesday. That was her regular day."

"Not Thursday, or Friday?" Julia was disappointed with his initial response.

"No, but I knew she was on the island on Thursday."

"How?"

"George called me from the boat shop about a cotter pin, but I didn't have the one she needed, or at least I couldn't find one." He shrugged as they both surveyed the crowded shop.

"Do you know anyone else on the island who might have seen her on Thursday or Friday?"

"She was very good friends with Constant Gumps, who owns the taxi business here."

"Yes, I know who he is. Where will I find him today?"

Germain looked at his watch. "At this time, he should be finishing up with afternoon tours. I would bet he will be at the dock by the catamarans in the next 15 minutes."

"Thank you so much. Merci! I should have thought of that myself!" Julia was excited as she headed toward the open door.

"Bien! I hope you can find him."

Julia was only a few hundred yards from the marina. She fairly ran to the area Germain had mentioned. It was the same place she

165

and the Gradys had first met Constant when they disembarked from the "El Tigre" several days earlier. There were already several dozen tourists congregated near the boats, waiting for the return trip to St. Maarten. She didn't see Constant anywhere, nor was his van in the lot.

The next few minutes passed slowly as Julia watched the crowd get larger. Finally, Julia spotted Constant's taxi-van. The red and white stripes were quite unique. She felt her heart rate increase with anticipation as she ran across the lot to the van.

Only a few seconds later, her excitement faded into disappointment when she saw that the driver was not Constant. "Excuse me, sir, where is Constant Gumps today?"

The young bearded man replied, "I'm not sure. He asked me to drive for him today because he had other business, but he didn't say where he would be. Perhaps I can help you." He had noticed the disappointment on Julia's face.

Julia brightened as she realized he might also have known Linda. "Maybe you can. This is Linda Townsend," she showed him her photo. "Did you see her last Thursday or Friday?"

His face darkened. "Why do you want to know?"

"I'm trying to find out if she mentioned going to her cave on the way home Thursday, or if she went on Friday instead. Did you see her last week?"

"What difference does it make? She's dead!"

"It makes 24 hours of difference! Were you friends with her?"

His face softened. "Yes, you could say that. I even loved her at one time. She was my wife until three years ago. I did see her Thursday, but I don't see how that helps you."

Julia was stunned. She hadn't expected to learn that Linda's ex-husband was on the island. "To tell the truth, I'm not exactly sure myself how or if it helps yet. Do you know anyone who might have wanted her killed?"

There were tears in his eyes as he answered quietly, "No. I'm sorry. I really can't help you."

Julia was speechless as he walked away. She finally regained her composure and turned away herself. She glanced at her watch and noted that she had less than 90 minutes to keep her date with Martin. She considered the chances of learning more on St. Bart's and decided to head back to St. Maarten.

She was more than halfway home when the engine started to sputter. Julia glanced at the gauges and dials. Nothing seemed out of order. She crossed her fingers and opened the throttle a bit. The sputtering stopped, and her anxieties eased. Suddenly, a loud "pop" pierced the air and the boat stalled in the water.

Julia knew instinctively that something major had happened. She turned off the ignition key and went to the back of the boat and raised the outboard motor. The propeller was mangled in a length of rope. "Oh great!" she muttered to no one in particular, as she began to untangle the mess. Her task was made more difficult by the awkward position from which she had to work.

About 20 long minutes later, she finally had the propeller free except for a couple of very tight knots that could not be undone by hand. Julia looked unsuccessfully for a knife on the deck. She then looked for a repair kit of some kind. She finally found a few tools, including a sorry-looking knife, in one of the benches inside the small cabin. It only took a few strokes to cut through the main mess and free the propeller. What surprised Julia was finding that the rope had been tied in a neat double knot to the shaft just above the prop, as though someone had done it intentionally. But for what purpose? Julia doubted it would be enough to cause an accident, although it was conceivable. More likely, it was meant to slow her down, and keep her from returning to St. Maarten. Somebody was very worried about something. The something had to be related to Linda, but who the somebody was, was still a mystery.

Julia quickly finished her task and started the motor again. She was grateful that it started immediately. As she raced across the shimmering blue water, she sorted through the incidents of the week. She suddenly realized that whoever was stalking her might not actually be after her. Could Jill be in more danger than she herself was? Jill's boat, Jill's tanks, a threat at Jill's house. Julia sensed that Jill was in danger even now as she hurried back to St. Maarten.

The motor began to sputter again. At first, only occasionally, then more severely, and then the motor stopped altogether. Julia felt a sense of helplessness as she checked the tank and confirmed that she was out of gas. She checked all the stowage areas for a spare can of fuel. She had been unsuccessful when she noticed another boat pulling alongside.

"Ahoy! Are you okay?" the skipper asked.

"Yes, but I seem to be out of gas. Do you have any extra?"

"Certainly. Let me help you." The skipper appeared to be the sole occupant of the boat. He was 40ish, deeply tanned with graying dark brown hair and beard, and somewhat paunchy on his 5'10" frame. He picked up his spare can and stepped onto Julia's boat. Julia turned toward the motor to help him. Suddenly, she felt something warm and foul-smelling over her nose and mouth and was aware of a suffocating feeling. She struggled for a moment, then passed out.

CHAPTER EIGHTEEN

Sixteen Miles from Nowhere

Meanwhile, Greg and Martin waited for Julia at the Maho Reef Casino. It was already 6:15 P.M. and no one had seen Julia since that morning.

"Greg, are you sure you've thought of everyone who might have seen her?" Martin was a little worried, as was Greg.

"Yes. She called my office just before she left and said she was only planning an afternoon on St. Bart's. She wasn't going to the cave as far as I know. And Steve at the dive shop says she's not in yet."

"Well, she probably found herself in the middle of an adventure again!" Martin said, with a sarcastic sound in his voice.

Greg nodded. "That's what I'm afraid of. She doesn't have enough street sense to recognize danger when it stares her in the face. It's also not like her to fail to keep an appointment. She's always been quite prompt with me."

"That bothers me, too. I'm seriously considering sending someone out to intercept her."

Greg nodded again. "I had the same thought. She's an hour late now, and I know she intended to be here so she could prove to you and me that someone would break into her room while she was gone. So, where is she?" Greg was visibly concerned.

"What about Ian? Could she be with him?"

"No. He had some business this afternoon and gave me a message for her about tonight. In fact, that's why I'm here instead of him. He'd be worried if he knew she wasn't here yet."

Martin hit his left palm with his fist. "Well, I'm worried. I think we better go find her."

"I'm with you. Let's go."

• • •

Julia was aware of a pounding headache when she finally came to. Her watch said 6:20 P.M.. She was officially late for her meeting with Martin. She quickly assessed her surroundings. She was obviously on the water, judging from the sounds outside and the view from the port hole. She could see several other boats, all of which seemed to be smaller than the one she was on. She guessed that based on the size of the cabin in which she was confined. She couldn't see any land in the direction she could see, which was north and west, by the sunset toward her left. She figured she'd been unconscious one hour or longer.

She surveyed the cabin. She saw two single bunks, a small table, three dilapidated chairs, and several extra mismatched cushions for the chairs. The room seemed quite spacious, with a color scheme of blue and white with rose accents here and there. She particularly noticed that the room had a feminine atmosphere about it.

The sound of a key in the door brought Julia back to her senses. A surly dark-haired huge man with a full beard and a big gun walked in.

"Don't worry. I won't move," Julia volunteered.

"Doesn't matter. Nowhere you can go from here. We're miles from land. Would you like to be our guest for a short while?" The question sounded more like a sneer than an invitation.

"Who are you? What do you want from me?" Julia replied angrily.

"None of your business, Pretty One. We will soon be done and on our way and you'll be taken care of then." His body shook as he laughed.

"Who are you? What do you mean? I want to talk to the captain!" Julia tried being more forceful.

"Well, he doesn't want to talk to you just yet. You'll see him soon enough."

Julia could tell she would get nowhere with this guy. "Where am I?" She tried another tack.

"About sixteen miles from nowhere." With that, he grinned and turned to walk out, closing the door behind him.

Julia considered her predicament. Martin and Greg would be wondering where she was, but if they chose to try to find her, how would they know where to look? She sighed as she heard the "click" of the key in the door, locking her in again.

• • •

Greg and Martin had called Jon, who owned the local air service, and who was now flying them over the water route between St. Maarten and St. Barthelemy. They all searched for Julia's borrowed boat. Greg spotted it first, about ten miles offshore. Jon buzzed the small craft. They saw no sign of life aboard from the aircraft.

"Do you want me to land so you can check inside the cabin?" Jon asked.

Martin, who was using the binoculars, replied, "I can see pretty well. She's not on board. Can you get the customs office on your radio phone? Jon, let's turn back to the island."

Less than a minute later, Martin was on the line with Phillipe, Customs Senior Officer. "Phillipe, we have a problem. Jon, Greg and I are going to have to make a move earlier than we'd planned. Can you get your men set to go one hour earlier?"

"Mais, oui! So, we rendezvous at 9:30 instead of 10:30?"

"Yes, same place as planned."

"Martin, can you tell me what the problem is?"

"I'm really not sure, but I think our little lady detective friend is in real trouble this time, and it looks like we have to go rescue her." Martin's voice had an edge of irritation.

"Yes, sir. Are all the plans the same except for the time?"

"Yes, Phillippe. Nine-thirty at Bluebird Point."

"Roger and out." Phillipe signed off.

"Well, Greg, it looks like we have to climb on our white chargers and rescue the damsel in distress. Are you ready?"

"Yes, Martin, but I'm worried. If she was kidnapped by Robert's men, she could be in real danger. How I wish she had dropped the detective stuff before things got to this point." Greg was obviously very concerned.

"Yes, Greg. I know. I'm worried too, but there's nothing we can do for now. We'll have to go through with Bluebird and hope for the best." Martin looked at Greg and they nodded at each other.

CHAPTER NINETEEN

Out of Petrol?

Julia had ascertained to her unhappy satisfaction that there was no way out of the cabin in which she was being held prisoner. At this point, she had not yet determined who her captors were, though she felt a strong sense of fear. These guys didn't seem to be amateurs.

Time passed slowly.

At about 7:30, the door was unlocked again. This time a young woman came in. She, too, was armed. She also bore a strong resemblance to Sheila, enough so that Julia commented on it.

"Sheila is my sister. Some people think we're twins but she's two years older than I am."

"What do you want with me?" Julia asked this new face.

"We need your help tonight."

"What kind of help?" Julia was very curious.

"A little diversionary routine. I'll tell you what to do." She casually tossed her long hair back over her shoulder.

"I don't understand."

"When we board the other boats, it helps to have a pretty woman to distract the men." She smiled, rather seductively.

"What other boats?" Julia was now both curious and confused.

"Don't ask me so many questions. You'll see very soon. I'll be back to get you in ten minutes. My name is Teresa, by the way." With that, she exited, locking the door behind her.

A short while later, Teresa and the gun-toting sailor returned for Julia and motioned for her to go with them. The three of them joined five or six other men on a 24-foot cabin cruiser. Julia was instructed to stay in the cabin until she was told to come outside. She did exactly that, along with the five men with guns. It seemed like quite a long while before the boat slowed down. "Julia, come out now," Teresa called to her. "Now, smile and be friendly. We're going to be invited to board the other boat. You don't do anything crazy, or I'll shoot you." She showed her handgun to Julia as she slid it into her pocket.

The other boat was a yacht at least 60 feet long, and luxuriously beautiful. The man who had feigned her rescue from Jill's boat was in command of the 24-foot boat. Julia had heard him addressed as "Sam."

"Ahoy, Sir. We're having a bit of trouble. Have you any spare petrol?" Sam asked the skipper of the yacht.

The bronzed man in his 50's on the deck of the yacht replied, "Certainly! Glad to help you out. Come on aboard!"

Sam motioned to Teresa and Julia as he climbed the ladder to the deck of the yacht. Teresa pushed Julia ahead of her and up they went.

Teresa and Julia's task was to find out the number of people on the boat as Sam talked with the skipper. Teresa chatted easily with the two women in the main cabin. Julia remained quiet. She knew she was a pawn and that any false move could be deadly. Teresa was able to determine that there were only two couples aboard. She called to Sam, "Was that two days in Phillipsburg, or four?"

As soon as she'd said that, two of Sam's men came into the cabin, showed their guns and directed the women outside onto the deck. Sam had taken charge of the two men outside already. The two men and two women were forced onto the smaller boat that Sam's crew had just left. In less than two minutes, Sam had taken over the yacht, without firing a gunshot.

He gave last minute advice to the displaced couples. "Don't waste the gas. You have just enough to get to land, at 180 degrees magnetic. I do hope you have a compass!" He laughed maliciously.

Julia felt very bad for the helpless people, but she was in no position to help them herself at this point. Julia was hustled into the main cabin where Teresa continued to keep her hand in the pocket with the gun. The trip back to their originating point was a bit circuitous in Sam's attempt to confuse anyone trying to follow or track him. Thus, it seemed longer than the trip out, at least to Julia.

Everyone aboard the mother ship, as Julia thought of it, was excited to see the magnificent yacht that Sam had captured.

"That's a gem, Sam. Mr. Roberts will be happy with this one. Good work!" Julia finally dared to ask Teresa what their operation was all about as she was escorted back to her "prison."

"You mean you haven't figured it out yet? And I thought you were pretty smart." Teresa was quite boastful as she explained to Julia, "Sam steals these big boats so Mr. Roberts can use them to smuggle drugs between Venezuela and St. Maarten."

"Why St. Maarten instead of the United States?"

"The U.S. would be too risky, because these boats are often from the U.S. and the officials are looking for them once they're reported stolen. It's not as big a problem down here in the Caribbean."

"So, how do the drugs get into the U.S.?" Julia continued with her questions.

"They're hidden in boxes of electronics such as radios and stereos and shipped to a warehouse in New York. I don't know what happens there."

"Who is this Mr. Roberts?"

"He is a very rich man. Very, very, rich." Teresa rolled her eyes. "And he pays very well. He'll be here later tonight, in fact. Right now we have a very large shipment and he's worried because something went wrong last week when he wasn't here. He doesn't want that to happen again."

"I'll bet not," Julia replied, a little sarcastically.

"He is also very interested in you." Teresa practically glared at Julia. "Me? Why?" Julia was quite surprised.

"He thinks you know something about the girl who died in the cave last week."

That caught Julia's interest, but she replied nonchalantly, "Not really, but why would it matter if I did?"

"She was a friend of his. He wants to know what you know."

"Does he think she was murdered, too?"

Teresa looked at Julia very closely before she replied, "No. Look, I have work to do. You will have to stay in this cabin until later. You can call me by pressing 7 on the intercom and saying, 'This is Julia. I need Teresa'. Someone will come and find me. You'll find some warmer clothes in that large drawer," she continued as she pointed to the inner wall. "I'll come for you in about an hour."

"And then what?"

"You'll see. It's kind of a surprise." Teresa smiled, and left the room, locking the door behind her.

Julia felt quite certain that she would not like the surprise. She was undoubtedly an expendable item and knew far too much to be set free. Julia needed to find a way to get off the boat, or radio for help without being caught. But first, she had to get out of the room.

CHAPTER TWENTY

Operation Bluebird

"Bluebird Command, Bluebird Command. Robin calling Bluebird Command," Greg said into the microphone.

"Yes, Robin. Go ahead." Martin's voice came through clearly.

"Bluebird, we're all set to go. We have six choppers ready to leave when you give the word."

"Understood. I think we have them on radar, but we're at least ten miles away still. I don't want to alert them yet until we get into position. Chickadee, what's your position?"

"About eight miles SSE of the target, Bluebird."

"Okay, stay where you are, Chickadee. Circle if necessary. We'll plan to converge at 2130. The scout plane showed nine boats, but the 100-footer is most likely the one we're after. Chickadee, is Ian with you?"

"No, Sir. He said he'd be on one of the other seaplanes. Do you want me to find him?"

"No, that's okay. I just wanted to know that he did at least get on a plane."

"Yes, Bluebird. He's up here somewhere. Chickadee clear."

"Okay, Chickadee. Robin, I want you to plan back up at 2135. Any questions?"

"Roger, we copy. 2135. Robin clear."

Greg turned to the helicopter pilot. "Well, I've got a date with Julia. Looks like we better go pick her up." He grinned as the pilot winked.

* * *

Julia knew she had to get out of her cabin for any chance at an escape. She hoped she could convince Teresa that her 'seasickness' was so severe that getting out on the deck was necessary.

Teresa was at her door within two minutes of calling on intercom "7." Julia was moaning and groaning with "sweat" rolling down her forehead when Teresa entered the room.

"What's the problem, Miss Fairchild?"

"I'm so sick. This cabin is giving me claustrophobia and making my seasickness worse." Julia moaned as if in pain.

"You only have 30 more minutes to wait here." She turned to leave.

"But I can't stand another 30 minutes. I think I'd be okay if I could just have a few minutes of fresh air on deck. Please." Julia did her best to look pale and wan.

"Well, okay. But you'll be watched all the time, so don't make any unfortunate moves." Teresa motioned Julia toward the door with her gun.

Julia stepped out the door and turned down the hall toward the stern. "Turn here, to the right," Teresa commanded.

Julia breathed in the fresh air as her heart started pounding.

"Go up to the deck and take a seat." Teresa's voice interrupted her racing thoughts.

Julia looked over every square inch of the part of the deck that she was on. The only sure exit was toward the bow, but one big black man with a gun stood in the aisle with his back to Julia. Julia knew the rear door went toward the cabins. She did not want to get stuck down there with Teresa. A pelican flying overhead caught her attention when its shadow shaded her momentarily. Although it was late in the evening, there was still a bit of the sun in the sky. As she looked up, she noticed a short ladder hanging from an upper deck that was otherwise inaccessible from Julia's position. She would have to jump to reach it but once there, she could have more options for finding a way to freedom.

The sound of footsteps behind her jolted her attention to her immediate predicament. She turned to find Teresa checking on her.

"Like I said, you're being watched. I would not want to be responsible, if you choose to do something stupid." Teresa spoke with a sharp edge to her voice. Julia merely nodded. As soon as Teresa was out of sight beyond the black guard, Julia moved closer to the ladder. This area of the deck measured about 20 by 30 feet with an open rail toward starboard, and a wall with no doors on port side. Stern-wise, a doorway led to the cabins below. The ladder was toward the bow, and it provided an access to the upper deck about ten feet above. The deck itself was open to the sky. The sun was quickly setting in the west, so the sunlight's reflections were quite bright off the water and the metal on the boat.

Julia spotted a small brass plaque and took it off the wall and slid it into her pocket. She moved a small stool from under a table to a new position beneath the ladder and stepped up. She took a big breath and grabbed the lower rung from the stool. She pulled herself up slowly, grateful for her arm exercises from her aerobics class.

She was able to reach the second rung with a lot of stretching. Her mind flashed back to the days of playing on the jungle gym in the grade school play yard. She reflected that horizontal ladder swinging was much easier than climbing up this vertical ladder.

The seconds passed slowly as she pulled all her weight up to the third rung. She still couldn't quite get her foot onto the lowest rung of the ladder, but was able to get a partial foothold on the wall itself. More precious seconds slipped by as she quietly grunted her way to the fourth rung, where she was finally able to get her knee onto the bottom rung.

She scrambled the last few rungs to the upper deck and surveyed her new surroundings. It didn't take long to figure out that going toward the bow was the way to go, and so Julia went.

She seemed to be close to midship as near as she could tell, and on the second highest deck. From her new position, she could see all the other boats surrounding the huge yacht, presently her prison. The sun was almost gone. Julia glanced at her watch and noted the time. It was almost 9:15. She could count on 15 to 20 minutes of twilight before being somewhat protected by darkness although the yacht was well-lit. Her immediate need was a hiding place until she could make a break. Even though it seemed like an obvious choice to look, even to her, Julia found herself considering the lifeboat about 20 feet ahead.

A few milliseconds later, Teresa's voice calling "Julia" in a harsh tone alerted Julia to move quickly, into the lifeboat. Julia scarcely breathed in her cramped quarters as Teresa and her cohorts approached, having figured out that she had climbed up the ladder. Julia hoped no one would notice the slight swaying of the lifeboat caused by her hasty entrance. It was a long minute before Teresa's gang moved on. Their voices and footsteps became quieter as they took their search toward the bow. Julia checked her watch. Only seven minutes had passed. She didn't believe she would have enough protection from the darkness until at least 9:30. She hoped she wouldn't be discovered for another few minutes at least, until darkness was in her favor.

Teresa and the three men with her were quite upset when they entered the main control rom. "Damn! She's on this boat! She can't be that hard to find!" Teresa slammed her gun down on the map table.

"Okay, Teresa. She's on the boat. Now, let's forget about her for the next little while and get our work done. We can find her and punish her later. It's more important right now to get ready for the chopper."

"Yes, Sam." Teresa sulked a little at the reprimand.

The sound of a chopper nearby broke the uncomfortable atmosphere. Everyone moved toward the chopper pad on the uppermost deck.

• • •

"Robin, Robin. Please come in, Robin. This is Bluebird calling." Martin's voice came over the radio as Greg glanced at his watch.

"Yes, Bluebird, this is Robin. Go ahead."

"We've just spotted a single chopper flying toward the main yacht. It looks like he knows where he's going."

"We copy. He's a little early. Maybe it's a good thing we changed our plans. Rendezvous as planned?"

"Roger, Robin. We'll alert you if it looks like he's leaving early."

"Roger, Bluebird. See you at 2130. Robin clear."

• • •

Julia heard the chopper approaching from her hiding place. Her watch said 9:25. She got up enough courage to peek out over the edge to see if she could see anything. She could hear a lot of shouting. Sam's voice was clear, even over the noise of the helicopter's blades. No one seemed to be close to her, so Julia decided to leave the lifeboat and get closer to the activity.

She scampered across the deck to the shelter of a hallway and surveyed the options. The helicopter pad was aft. The main control cabin was foredeck. The radio equipment had to be near the main cabin. She reasoned that her only chance of escape was to contact Ian or Martin. She sneaked across the edge of the deck and down the starboard side of the yacht toward the bow. She was thankful for the activity on the chopper pad because it gave her this opportunity. Much to her relief, there seemed to be no one in the radio room.

She quickly switched the frequency to Channel 16 and spoke quietly into the microphone. "Calling Martin Thompson. Calling Martin Thompson. Come in please. This is Julia, Martin. Come in please. This is Julia."

Julia head her breath as she paused for a response.

"Julia, this is Greg. Turn to Channel 9. Over."

"Copy. Turning to Channel 9." Julia switched to the designated channel.

"Greg, I'm so glad you heard me. I'm in trouble."

"So what else is new? What kind of trouble are you in this time?"

"I'm being held prisoner on a yacht somewhere off St. Maarten. I can't get off the boat! I'm scared!"

"Okay, Julia. I'll put someone on surveillance. Give us five minutes to find you."

"Oh, Greg. You don't know how happy I am to hear your voice."

"Julia, go hide until we get there. No more detective stuff. Do you copy?"

"I copy. Over. Hurry!"

As Julia put the microphone down, she felt cold metal against the back of her neck.

"And just what do you think you're doing?" asked Teresa.

"Would you believe I was ordering a pepperoni pizza for dinner?" Julia responded without moving a muscle.

"Whatever. It won't do you any good. We can't trust you now, so you'll have to stay with me until we're done." She motioned with the gun for Julia to go ahead of her. "Go to the left. You'll want to meet Mr. Roberts."

"You're sure about that?" Julia queried.

"Smart alecks have no place on this boat. Just move."

Julia and Teresa joined the group of men on the upper deck. Julia gasped when she saw who Sam was talking with.

"Tony!" Julia exclaimed.

Teresa turned to Julia, surprised. "Do you know Mr. Roberts?"

"No, I know 'Tony' as Mr. Romero. What is he doing here?"

"He runs the operation. We all work for him. You didn't know?"

"No, of course not."

Just then Tony came toward Julia and Teresa. "Well, Miss Fairchild. Fancy meeting you here."

"Tony, how could you be doing this?" Julia was stunned.

"Honey, it's called money, and I like money."

"So now what are you going to do with me?"

"Well, I really didn't plan to have to do anything, but unless we can make some special arrangements, we might have to have an 'accident.'"

"Like Linda's 'accident?'"

"Hey, now I didn't have anything to do with that."

"But you do know about it."

"I was informed. My people keep up with all the news."

Sam interrupted the conversation at that point. "We only have five more minutes to get out of here. Mr. McDonnell is ready when you are!"

CHAPTER TWENTY-ONE

"Will the Real Bad Guy Please Stand Up?"

"Ian?" Julia asked, incredulous.

Her question was answered when Ian stepped out of one of the rooms off the deck into the light.

"Ian! I can't believe this!"

"Well, hello, Beautiful! It's a small world, isn't it?" Ian grinned broadly.

"What are you doing here?" Julia demanded.

"It's called money, Love. Lots of money."

"Ian, I don't know what to say. This blows me away. I still can't believe you're mixed up in this. Is Greg involved, too?"

"No. This is one of my moonlighting adventures. I'm afraid I can't trust Greg to keep his mouth shut, so he knows nothing about this."

"So why have you been helping me this week?" Julia asked, still shocked.

"Helping you? How about calling it *watching* you? Tony couldn't be here, so he had me try to keep you out of trouble. A difficult task, I might add." Ian grinned again.

"So now what will you do with me? Am I expendable, like Linda?"

"Hey, I had nothing to do with Linda! Believe me," he added after a brief pause, "we will find something for you, I am sure."

"An accident, according to Tony." Julia spat the words out.

"Maybe not an accident." Ian countered.

Julia shuddered as she considered possible fates. Even though she'd talked with Greg, she really didn't have any hope at this moment that he would find her or be able to help her. She was very frightened.

Teresa poked her gun in Julia's ribs just then. "Okay, Miss Fairchild. We need to keep you out of trouble for a while."

Julia looked at Ian, as if looking for some assistance or reassurance from him. He was already engrossed in conversation with Tony. She knew she was in desperate straits. She was wishing she'd gone to Hawaii for her vacation instead of St. Maarten.

Teresa nudged Julia into the main control room, and then into a small room off to the port side. Teresa closed and locked the door from the outside. Just as the lock clicked, the sound of helicopters filled the air. Julia's heart soared. Teresa hurried to the deck.

Outside, Sam's men took up their positions as the helicopters neared. "Hold fire," Sam yelled, "until I signal."

The sky was filled with helicopters…five in all. One was approaching the helicopter pad when Sam gave the signal. Shot after shot rang out, from the yacht as well as the choppers. The first chopper touched down and 6 men scrambled off.

Julia could only see part of what was going on, but she could hear all the guns very clearly. She was trying not to think about what might happen next. She kept trying the door knob as if it would somehow magically be unlocked if she tried just one more time. Suddenly the door *did* open, and Julia fell back as lost her balance, only to be helped by Tony Roberts-Romero.

"You're coming with me," he growled.

Julia was too frightened to resist as he pulled her behind him toward the door. The shooting had stopped, Julia noticed. When Tony got to the door of the main control room, he stopped and pushed Julia in front of him.

"Okay, Thompson, you've gone far enough. You let me go, and I'll let the lady go. You can have the yacht and everything here. I'll leave quietly and never come back. What do you say?" Tony had his left arm under Julia's chin and held a gun in her ribs with his other hand.

Martin stood about 20 feet away with several of his men. Julia scanned the area. She noticed that most of the men from the "mother ship" appeared to be under guard.

"Sorry, Roberts, but I'm holding the cards this time. You're out of aces. I'm sure you don't want to add murder to the charges. Let Julia go." Martin was taking charge, to Julia's delight.

"Not until you guarantee that I can leave." Tony kept the gun in Julia's ribs.

"Can't do that. Let her go."

Just then there was a loud crash above Julia's head. She looked up to find Ian standing on the upper deck, holding a gun on Martin.

"Tony, I'll cover while you come up here. Martin, I promise I'll shoot you and Julia if you make a false move. Call your men off and let him go."

Martin looked at Julia, being held by Tony, and then up at Ian. He appeared to be weighing the options. After a long moment, he said simply, "You can go."

Tony pushed Julia ahead of him toward Ian, who helped Julia scramble to the top of the deck. Ian held cover as Tony then followed. The three of them then ran to the waiting helicopter. At the last instant, when Julia thought she would be released, she instead found herself being pushed into the chopper by Tony.

"Let me go, please!" she cried.

"Sorry, Sweetheart. You're too high-risk. You're coming with us."

"Tony, we don't need her," Ian interrupted.

"She just might come in handy. Besides, she's always fun. I might use her to keep the bed warm, if nothing else," Tony added with a sneer.

"Tony, leave her here. She doesn't deserve to be hurt."

"McDonnell, when did you start getting soft? She comes with us!" Tony gripped Julia's arm even harder.

In reality, it was too late to do anything anyway as the helicopter was already in the air and moving to the southwest. The pilot deftly guided the craft at low altitude over the water.

After a few minutes, Julia couldn't stand the relative silence. "Ian, why did you get mixed up in this?"

"Julia, I don't think you'd understand just now."

"Was Jill in on this, too?"

"Not on purpose, no."

"So, somehow Linda got involved and had to be silenced. And now you're going to have to do something with me. Am I reading the script correctly?"

"Like I said, Julia, you wouldn't understand right now." Ian looked at her apologetically.

"Well, I understand that Sheila's sister Teresa works for you two. Maybe that expensive car that Sheila is driving was paid for by illegal money. Maybe it really belongs to Teresa. That seems to make some sense. And I understand that Jill's tanks were substituted for Linda's tanks when they were retrieved so they would be reported as normal. And I understand that you had a key to Linda's house and could have made the switch. And you always knew where I was. And Greg is so easy-going, he was helping you keep track of me and probably didn't even know you were using both of us."

"Wait a minute! It sounds like you're accusing me of quite a few things. Don't I deserve a fair hearing?" Ian threw up his hands.

"And you, Mr. Roberts or Romero, or whatever. You used me, too. You probably knew all along that Linda wouldn't be there, and you played with my life!"

Tony replied, "Actually, Linda's misfortune was an ill-timed accident. That was supposed to happen *after* she met you at the airport. She was becoming a liability to our enterprise. So, then we had the problem of getting the papers from you. You caused a bit of a delay by being so uncooperative. I am sorry that we have had to cause you any discomfort or concern, but there are reasons."

Just then the pilot interrupted. "Mr. Roberts, we shall have to land at St. Kitts and refuel. We cannot make it to Curacao otherwise."

"Go ahead and stop. We don't seem to have any chasers behind us."

Julia was afraid for her life, but still had unanswered questions. "What about Scott? Why was he killed? Did he know too much, too?"

"Well, he didn't know as much as he thought he did, but he was itching to tell the wrong people, and it just wasn't convenient for us to have him spill the beans yet," Ian replied.

"Okay, so here we are. Julia, you'll stay with me, so I can keep an eye on you. Tony, I'll make a phone call and give them our ETA."

As soon as the chopper touched down on the ground, Ian was out the door, pulling Julia with him. They hurried into the small building nearby.

"Julia, it's not how it looks, but I'll explain later. You just wait for me right here. This man will take care of you." He motioned to a burly young man behind the counter. "I have to go take care of Tony."

Julia looked at the man Ian indicated. To her surprise, it was one of the men she'd seen in Martin's office on one occasion. She was now totally confused. She watched Ian go back outside toward the helicopter. When he was still ten yards away, he raised his left arm and twenty or more men appeared from nowhere.

The helicopter started to lift off, but before it got 30 feet into the air, something hit the blade and put the craft into a dive to the ground. The ensuing explosion made a deafening noise, and flames leaped into the sky almost immediately. Julia burst into tears then as she reacted to her own near-disaster.

. . .

"It's okay, Julia. It's all over now." Greg's voice broke through the tears and sobs as he hugged her.

"Greg! How did you get here?"

"It's a long story. Right now, let's all get back to St. Maarten. I do still owe you a dinner tonight, after all!"

"You really are my knight in shining armor!" Julia let herself melt into Greg's strong arms as they walked to another waiting helicopter.

. . .

Later, after a meal and wine shared with Jill and the Gradys, Julia, Ian, Greg and Martin related details about what had happened. Julia shared that she wanted to trust them all, but kept finding discrepancies in what they told her, compared to what she thought.

Julia continued, "And I really wasn't certain about Martin. Intellectually, I wanted to believe he was doing all the right things, but my gut feeling was that he was trying to keep this covered up. Ian seemed very credible for the most part, which may be why he was able to infiltrate Tony's operation. He certainly had me fooled!" Julia turned to smile at Ian, who pretended to be hurt by her comment.

"What was it that made you decide Linda was murdered?" Jill broke in, happy to share the joy in Julia's safe recovery.

"Remember when we went into the cave the second time?"

Jill nodded, her face serious.

"I found a metal tag with Linda's tank number on it. And it didn't match the tanks Martin had in his office. So, I knew there'd been a switch, but when and where, I wasn't sure."

"So, you suspected me," Martin said, a little sarcastically.

"Not exactly. I thought maybe you were being bamboozled, or perhaps you were trying to put me off. Anyway, I found the records at the dive shop for the "real" set of tanks, the "murder weapon," so to speak. I discovered that Scott had checked them in and out. He may have known that they were "doctored" with exhaust, which can be done fairly easily, if you know how, and threatened blackmail." Julia paused to take a breath.

"Doctored by whom?" This was Jill again.

"Sheila, maybe. She had access and some motivation, since she was Tony's new girl. And she'd been diving with Linda previously, so it wouldn't be too unusual for her to get Linda's tanks refilled. She was probably the lousy poet as well." Julia glanced at Martin to see if he was going to offer any additional information.

Martin had been listening intently and now took over the conversation with the next question. "Julia, what about those papers you had for Linda? Did you know what they were? They were from Tony, weren't they?"

"Yes, they were from Tony, but I had no way of knowing there was anything unusual about them until my room was broken into. Tony told me they were important, but not why, and to keep them safe."

Ian interrupted. "But did you suspect Tony in any way?"

"Not really, although I was curious enough to open the package after the second note and the break-in. But I didn't think of it as anything illegal at the time. It was just a bunch of numbers."

"Julia, why was it so important to you personally to go after Linda's murderer?" Ian asked.

Julia paused for a few seconds before answering. "I felt responsible...like I was the intermediary, and I wanted to vindicate myself."

"But no one ever implied that you were responsible!" Martin exclaimed.

"That's true, but somehow I still felt responsible. I also was worried about Jill. A thought occurred to me that she might be the real target. After all, someone broke into her house. Then, I had her boat and her tanks the day I was almost snuffed out, and I thought I may have just been in the wrong place at the wrong time." Julia shrugged her shoulders with that explanation and paused to take a couple of swallows of her drink.

Julia continued. "In fact, I suspected Jill for a while. She knew where I was much of the time, and I thought she might be feeding information to someone."

Jill glanced at Julia with a surprised look.

"I suspected Greg, too, I'm afraid. Especially when he showed up at my side more often than I would expect by chance. But then I decided it was more likely that Martin had told him to shadow me. I really wanted to trust Greg and, in the end, he's the one I trusted the most. I'm not sure if that was my sixth sense." Julia gave him a very warm smile. "Or those blue eyes!"

Several of the group laughed, especially Greg.

Greg finally said, "I was shadowing you, but at Ian's instructions. Even Martin didn't know all of Ian's hand, and I was busy trying to cover for him, while keeping you out of trouble, and try to appear innocent at the same time!" Greg chuckled again. With a softer voice he added, "I do really like you, you know."

Julia looked at him with a sweet smile. "Thank you for rescuing me, again and again. You are my favorite knight!" She kissed him on the cheek with that.

She then interrupted the moment with a question. "Martin, how did it help you to know I was looking for Linda? Or was it something else that helped?"

"We had been aware for some time of a connection between the boat pirating and drugs, and we had some intel that the big boss might be in Boston. It was more of an educated guess than actual hard evidence that the papers you had for Linda from Boston might be a key to the boat pirating scheme. As it turns out, Sheila and Steve were both involved as well. Although we had the Bluebird project planned for tonight anyway, it was a lucky accident that we moved up the time when you turned up missing."

Martin was smiling at Julia now. "Otherwise, we might have missed this opportunity. Julia, I do thank you for your part in nailing Tony Roberts-Romero, and I apologize for giving you so much grief this week." Martin extended his hand in a gesture of a truce.

Julia took his hand, then got up and gave him a big hug. "Thank *you*, for saving my life!"

"Julia, somehow I think you would have managed, but I am very glad you are safe."

The room was quiet for a moment, then Greg broke the silence. "I don't know about the rest of you, but I'm exhausted and I'm going to take Julia home." He turned to see if that was okay with Julia.

It was. She nodded her agreement.

"And I am going to offer Julia another week in the sun on our 'Friendly Island,' courtesy of our government, for helping us make this a safer place. Julia, can you stay?" Martin looked hopefully at Julia.

Julia considered for a moment how she would manage another week away from work. Then she turned to Greg and beamed, as she nodded 'yes' to Martin.

As Julia and Greg neared the door to leave, Julia turned around once more and said to Martin and Ian, with a broad grin:

"Roses are red.
The Ocean is blue.
Promise me no more rhymes,
And I'll stay with you."

ACKNOWLEDGEMENTS

First, I must thank my dear friend, Angela Thompson, for her editing skill, and helping me develop the covers for the e-book and paperback version. She found wonderful images and helped me hone just the right look. We sing together in our church choir, and "sang" together as well with this project.

Additional thanks to my sister Carleen and others who helped review and critique my manuscript.

An expert editor, Heather Snyder, found errors that others missed and helped improve my story with a few word changes here and there. Thank you! Any errors that remain are on me.

A master typist, Joanne Baker, did all the transcription work when I first wrote this story. I hope she is as happy as I am that it is finally a "real" book. Funny things happen, by the way, when a document in Word 97 is converted to Windows 10!

Just when I needed him, a new friend, Savan Kong, joined my circle of life. He was extremely helpful: teaching me about .epub, author's pages on Amazon.com and self-publishing in general. He was very gracious in his encouragement. Thank you!

Thank you to all my friends who let me babble on about my book over all these years. This is the year I will finally be able to say in my annual Christmas letter that I have published my novel!

Of course, thanks go to Rob Siders of 52Novels.com for formatting my book for e-publishing. I may be a great physician, but I am not as skilled in computers.

A special thanks to my husband, Steve, who has patiently witnessed all the steps necessary to get my story into print.

PJ Peterson

ABOUT THE AUTHOR

PJ Peterson loved to read mysteries as a young person. She followed the pursuits of Trixie Belden and Nancy Drew, later graduating to the mysteries by Agatha Christie and other notable authors. This is her debut novel in that mysterious realm.